THE BODYGUARD

THE BODYGUARD

THE NATE THROWER SERIES
BOOK 1

MIKE RYAN

WWW.MIKERYANBOOKS.COM

Copyright © 2023 by Mike Ryan

All rights reserved.

No part of this book may be reproduced in any form or by any electronic or mechanical means, including information storage and retrieval systems, without written permission from the author, except for the use of brief quotations in a book review.

Cover Design: The Cover Collection

1

Thrower walked slowly over to the bed and plopped down on it. It was a nice bed. The nicest one he'd seen in over a week. Thrower figured he'd earned it after what he'd been through over the past week. He didn't usually care about staying in expensive and luxurious hotels, but considering he'd been sleeping on floors and old cots on his latest job, he thought it was time to splurge a little.

Protecting people was what Thrower did best. His nickname was the Bodyguard. For some, that was all they knew him by. Especially the people that he went up against. He was a big man, with a military background, and well adept at fighting. He had to be, considering he was usually brought into situations that were not in his favor. But that was his specialty. Winning in spite of the odds. The clients who hired him usually had unique or extreme circumstances for doing so. He wasn't brought on board just to stand around looking tough when someone could hire a team of four others to do the same thing. No, Thrower was brought in when there was an extreme likelihood of violence.

Thrower was looking up at the ceiling and just barely closed his eyes when there was a knock on the door. He opened his eyes and lifted his head, looking over at the door. He then quickly sat up and got into defensive mode. He wasn't expecting anyone since his job was finished earlier in the day. He didn't call for room service. And he had no friends in the area that he was aware of.

He got off the bed and started walking toward the door, putting his hand on his waist to feel the gun that was attached to his leg. Maybe there was some unfinished business from his last job.

Thrower stood next to the door, making sure he wasn't in the way of any bullets that may pierce through it. He'd seen that movie before. He wasn't going to look through peepholes, and he wasn't going to say anything, not while standing directly behind a door. There were three more knocks on the door.

"Yes?" Thrower finally said.

"Nate Thrower?"

Thrower was silent for a moment, trying to quickly think of a name to match the man's voice. It wasn't one he recognized. "Depends on who's asking."

The Bodyguard

"My name is Carlos Espinoza. I have a business proposition for you. I understand you're for hire."

"Depends on the job."

"That is what I would like to talk to you about."

Thrower analyzed the man's voice. When you were thrust into the situations that he'd been in and to be the one walking out on top, you had to pick up on things like that. Sometimes, it was the little details that were the difference between life and death. In his experience, people had a certain way of talking, depending on the situation. Sometimes people hurried their words, some people's voices would crack, some would have their pitch go up and down, seemingly nervous about how those words would be perceived. And he usually had a pretty good indication of when people were lying.

This guy didn't sound like any of those. His voice seemed natural and calm. Thrower, feeling a little better about the situation, leaned over to look through the peephole. He saw a middle-aged man in a suit, and an expensive-looking one at that. There didn't appear to be anyone else with him.

Thrower put his hand on the door and unlocked it, then quickly pulled it open. He stayed to the side of the door for a few moments, just in case he had assessed the situation incorrectly. He hadn't, though. The man stood there in the doorway, waiting to be invited in. He thought the man known as the Bodyguard was acting a bit strange, but he'd been around erratic behavior before, so it wasn't exactly something new to him.

With nothing happening, Thrower finally showed his face.

"Nathan Thrower, I presume?"

"How do you know my name and where I was?"

The man grinned. "Well, when someone of your reputation arrives in an area, you should know that it doesn't take long for word to travel. Especially when one needs the services of someone like that."

"I take it that's you?"

Espinoza shook his head. "No. I'm here acting as a third party."

"I don't deal with third parties. I like to talk to the people who hire me directly."

"And you shall. I am only here to gauge your interest at first."

"You sound like a lawyer. Or a high-priced personal assistant. Which is it?"

Espinoza smiled again. "The latter. I am here on behalf of Mr. Manuel Ortiz. He has a need for your services."

"Don't know him." Thrower's eyes went past the man, looking into the hallway, clearly appearing like his attention was diverted. It wasn't unnoticed.

"Am I keeping you from something? Or am I interrupting something, perhaps?"

"No, I just finished a job earlier today." Thrower then flashed him a smile. "I just like to make sure there are no lingering bad feelings from anyone who might decide to get frisky."

"I see. In that case, would you mind if we discussed our business inside? That way I'm not feeling vulnerable out here? Just in case your fears become warranted."

"I suppose we could do that."

Thrower let him inside, closing the door and locking it behind him.

"You have good taste in accommodations, Mr. Thrower. I have stayed here many times. Excellent service here."

"I wouldn't know about that. I was more or just interested in not sleeping on the floor like I have been lately."

"I understand. I guess the first thing I should know is whether you're available at the moment?"

"Why don't you tell me what you need me for, and I'll tell you how available I am?"

"Fair enough. As I said, I represent Manuel Ortiz. He is the CEO of Ortiz & Vega, a quickly growing company here."

"When you say quickly growing, you mean what?" Thrower asked.

"I mean that it's a multi-million-dollar business, with the capability of making billions in a few years."

"I guess it's good work if you can find it."

"Indeed. As you may already know, being in charge of a company like this—that's starting to get recognized—comes with a lot of perks and benefits. But it also comes with pitfalls."

"Let me guess. Threats, extortion, kidnapping, things like that?"

"Exactly."

"So which is it?" Thrower asked.

"All of it. He's been told to pay a million dollars in a few days. If not, they threaten action."

"What kind of action?"

Espinoza shrugged. "We don't know. Nothing specific. They literally said if it wasn't paid, that they'd take action. No mention of what that action would be."

"And you think they might follow through with this threat?"

"I don't know. But I think we have to go with the belief that they would."

"Any thought to just paying it?" Thrower asked.

Espinoza made a face, indicating that wasn't an appealing proposition. "There have been other threats before. We've always ignored them."

"So what makes this one different?"

"This is the third one this group has made."

"Did they put a name on it? How do you know it's the same group?"

"They signed it the same way. Liberation."

"Liberation? What does that mean?"

Espinoza shrugged again. "Your guess is as good as ours."

"Is that some kind of terrorist group here?" Thrower asked.

"Not that we're aware of."

"You said this group made two other threats? Why'd you ignore the other ones?"

"Mr. Thrower, if you start capitulating to demands and threats all the time, you'll eventually go broke. They'll just keep coming back for more."

"Have you actually responded to any of these, or did you just put them in the trash?"

"We've never replied to anything." Espinoza reached into his pocket and removed some folded papers. He handed them to Thrower. "Here. I've brought the notes they sent us for you to look at. Maybe you see something we don't."

Thrower carefully looked at each of the three notes.

The first one read,

We want $250,000 or we will slowly dismantle your business. Bring the money, unmarked, to the address on the other side of this paper.

Liberation.

Thrower looked confused. It was an interesting way of phrasing things, he thought. He then put the note on the bottom of the pile and read the second one.

Since you ignored our first demand, we now want $500,000. Things will only get worse if you continue to ignore us. Bring the money, unmarked, to the address on the other side of this paper.

Liberation.

Thrower turned the paper over and looked at the address. It was the same as the first address. He then shuffled the note to the bottom and read the latest one.

We now want $1,000,000. Continuing to ignore us will not be good for you or your family. Their safety should be your utmost concern. We will take action if our demands are not met promptly.

Liberation.

Espinoza was right. There was something different about each of them. The last one seemed to have an angry tone to it. It definitely seemed to be escalating.

"Have you gotten anything else besides these?"

"No other letters or notes, no."

"What about phone calls? Knocks on the door? Flat tires? Rocks through a window? Anything like that? Anything that might be considered unusual or weirdly coincidental?"

Espinoza shook his head. "No, nothing that I'm aware of."

"What is it that Mr. Ortiz wants from me?" Thrower asked.

"Protection. That is the game you're in, is it not? I can assure you, you will be well paid for your efforts. Money is no object."

Money wasn't a chief concern for Thrower, but he usually didn't tell people that. Especially the people who could afford it. It was usually the people who couldn't afford him where the money was not an issue for him.

"What about Mr. Ortiz' family?"

"He has a wife and two small children. It is his top priority that they're protected."

"So what does he want from me? Protect him? His family? Both? What?"

"He is willing to put himself in your hands. Whatever you deem to be most appropriate."

Thrower scratched his face as he read the notes again. "I assume Mr. Ortiz already has his own security team?"

"He only employs two other men. Up until now, there has never been a need for more."

"You said there's been other threats before this?"

"Nothing that ever seemed as important as this."

"Is he dissatisfied with the men he's already got?" Thrower asked.

"He is of the belief that in a situation like this, the best should be acquired. And you do have that reputation."

"Lucky that I just happened to come along?"

Espinoza smiled. "Yes. Most fortunate."

"What would he have done if I didn't happen to be here?"

"He probably would have hired more men for the moment. And then contacted you in hopes of bringing you in. Now we don't have to go through all the trouble."

"He still might need to hire more men," Thrower said.

"You won't take the job?"

"Even if I do, I'm not a miracle worker. And I can't be in two places at once. Unless Mr. Ortiz is willing to hunker down with his family until this matter's resolved, I can't protect everybody."

"He is in charge of a major corporation. He is not about to hide out in fear. But he is willing to submit to whatever you think is best, other than staying in his bedroom for the next several months."

"If I agree to take the job, I'm in charge. I'll protect people my way."

"Of course."

"But my job isn't to find out who's behind this or investigate in any way. I don't do that unless I just happen to stumble upon it. My only job is to protect who I'm supposed to. And I'll do that to the best of my ability and my dying breath."

"I understand."

"So hiring me only gets rid of half the problem."

"Half?"

"Like I said, I can protect people all day long. Unless they attack, and I get rid of all of them in the process, there's still the matter of finding out who's doing it in the first place. That has to be understood."

"It is. Perfectly."

"But I still won't accept anything until I've talked to him myself."

"He's ready whenever you are."

Thrower shrugged. "Guess I'm ready now."

"Great. I have a car downstairs, ready and waiting."

"No offense, but I have a rental. I'll drive myself. I tend not to trust anybody until I'm hired."

"Of course. I understand your precaution. A man in your line must be careful. If you follow me, I'll lead the way."

Thrower went over to the table and grabbed his backup weapon, stuffing it in its holster on the back of his belt.

"Expecting trouble?"

Thrower shrugged. "Never can tell. But I also never leave without it. Sometimes, trouble just has a way of finding me."

2

As Thrower stopped in front of the gate just behind Espinoza's car, he couldn't help but look at the house behind it. It looked like a rather large estate. Espinoza stuck his arm out the window and typed in some sort of code on the box that was attached to the brick wall. A second or two later, the gate started to open. Espinoza drove onto the property, with Thrower following him.

They drove down a lengthy driveway, which circled around a water fountain, with a large statue in the center of it. They stopped right in front of the house. Espinoza got out of his vehicle first and walked over to Thrower's car, standing next to the door, waiting for his guest to step out.

Once Thrower did, his eyes were immediately drawn to the house.

"Beautiful house, isn't it?"

Thrower nodded. "Looks expensive."

Espinoza shrugged and threw his arms out. "Five thousand square feet. More bedrooms and bathrooms than are needed, and a pool out back that a luxurious hotel would be envious of. I told you, money would be no object here."

"It's not the money I worry about."

Espinoza held his arm out toward the house. "Let's go inside, shall we? Mr. Ortiz is eager to meet you."

"Lead the way."

The two men went inside, passing by what Thrower assumed to be a maid since she was tidying up the place. Thrower looked around the rooms as he passed through them, with Espinoza leading him to the back of the house. They stopped once they reached the sliding glass doors that led to the backyard.

Espinoza slid the door open and he stepped outside, with Thrower following closely. It was a large backyard, though the in-ground swimming pool appeared to be the main attraction. There was a diving board, a slide, and it was so big it looked like it belonged to an Olympic swimmer. The only person in the pool at this time was a bikini-clad woman, who was sitting on the steps in the shallow end, sipping an alcoholic drink.

There was another man nearby, sitting in a lounge chair, looking through a magazine. Thrower took a quick look around, expecting to see one of the other guards, though he didn't see anyone yet. He thought it was a little strange that the security was so light for someone who had been dealing with some threats.

Espinoza led Thrower right over to Ortiz. As soon as he saw them coming, Ortiz stood up and put the magazine on the chair.

Ortiz put his hand out to shake his guest's hand as he got closer. "Mr. Thrower, I presume?"

Thrower grinned and put his hand in Ortiz'. "That's me."

"Thank you for coming. I really appreciate it. When Carlos heard you were in town, he told me you were the man we needed. He's already explained the situation to you, correct?"

"Mostly. I'd like to hear it in your own words, though."

"Of course, of course. Before we get started, can I offer you a drink? I have a fully stocked bar. Anything you'd like."

"Thanks. Just water would be fine. I don't drink when I'm on a job or discussing business."

Ortiz pointed at him and laughed. "Smart man. Smart man. Nothing to cloud the judgment, right?"

"Something like that."

"Eva. Get our friend a drink here."

The woman in the pool slowly got out, with Ortiz admiring her figure as her body glistened from the beads of water still on her skin.

"Please, sit, sit." Ortiz held his hand out, pointing

The Bodyguard

towards a circular glass table that was only a few feet away from them.

The three men sat down.

"So, what can I tell you?"

"What do you know about this Liberation group?" Thrower asked.

"Nothing. Absolutely nothing. I've even checked in with the police, and they told me they haven't heard of them either."

"Are they actively working on it?"

Ortiz threw his arms up. "Who knows? Police here sometimes do things at their own discretion and their own pace. That is why I wanted extra protection. I do not know if I can count on them."

"Carlos told me you already had a couple of guards," Thrower said. "But I don't see them anywhere."

"Oh, one is out front, roaming around. The other is in the house. No need to have them back here. I am adequately protected here."

The woman came over to the table, several drinks in her hand. A bottle of water for Thrower, a drink for both Ortiz and Espinoza, and one for herself.

"Join us, my dear," Ortiz said, pulling out a chair next to him. "This is my wife, Eva." Ortiz thought he detected a certain look on Thrower's face, apprehensiveness about discussing the details of the job. "If you're worrying about watching what you say, there is no need. Eva knows all about what is going on. I have already discussed it with her."

"And you have children?"

"Two. A boy and a girl. They are nine and seven."

Thrower looked around. "Are they here?"

"No, they are with their mother at the moment." Thrower's eyes quickly glanced at Eva. Ortiz let out a laugh. "Eva is my second wife. The children's stepmother."

"So they don't live here full time, then?"

"No. I only get them on weekends. Can you believe that? I'm worth a fortune, I have this mansion, an important job, and I can only see my children on weekends? Such a travesty."

"That could be problematic, don't you think?"

Ortiz threw his arms up. "Yes, perhaps."

"Does their mother know about this?"

"I have not yet told her, no."

"Don't you think you should?"

"I do not want to upset her unnecessarily. I'll never hear the end of it. I'm sure she would use it as an excuse to give me even less time with the children."

"I try not to butt into people's private lives, but... when you get a note literally saying the safety of your family is at stake, I think you better take it seriously."

Ortiz sighed and put both of his hands over his face, rubbing it up and down. "I try not to give that woman any extra ammunition."

"If you believe this threat is real, which I gather you

do since I'm here, you should be doing everything possible to protect anyone who means something to you."

"What should I do?"

Thrower looked around. "You've got a large place here, right? What about moving them in for a couple of weeks until this blows over?"

Ortiz laughed. It was small at first, then grew into a bigger belly laugh. "You're joking, right? You must be joking."

Thrower looked at him stoically. He then shook his head. "Nope."

"Then you mean just moving my children in?"

"Why not?"

"Because you don't know their mother, my friend. She is a mean, vindictive woman. Ask anyone. She won't let the children stay with me one second longer than they are required to. It is ridiculous."

"Then have her stay too."

Ortiz smiled at first, then laughed even harder than the first time. "I've heard of your reputation, but I didn't realize you were such a comedian. That was not in your profile."

"I'm not joking," Thrower said.

"You want my children and my ex-wife to stay here for a couple of weeks? With me and my current wife? Surely you are not serious?"

"Look, I realize that having them stay may not be ideal. But you're not paying me under ideal circumstances. If you want you, your wife, and your children protected, I can't be in two or three places at once."

Ortiz sighed again, putting his hand over his mouth as he thought about it.

"I know it would be awkward," Thrower said. "I know it would be uncomfortable. I know it's not a perfect scenario. But if you believe this threat is as real as it sounds, then you're the one who needs to take it seriously."

Ortiz stared at him for a few moments, knowing what Thrower was telling him was probably the right thing to do. But it still wouldn't be easy to go through with it. He then grabbed his drink off the table and drank the rest of it, forcefully putting his glass back down. He then looked at his wife. She just shrugged, seemingly OK with whatever he decided.

"Carlos... what do you say?" Ortiz asked.

Espinoza glanced at his boss and friend for a moment, then looked at Thrower. "I think... I think you are paying him for his expertise. I think you should probably listen to his advice."

After a few more seconds, Ortiz nodded, looking as though he'd finally come to a resolution. "I will... I will tell her. I'll try to explain it to her and see if I can get her to come here with the children."

"Try hard," Thrower said. "Make sure she knows what's at stake."

"I will. It will not be pleasant, either the conversation, or, God forbid, her staying here again. But we must all do unpleasant tasks from time to time, don't we?"

"Definitely do."

"As for your payment, I was thinking five thousand American dollars per week."

Thrower grimaced slightly. Though money was never a motivating factor in whether he took a job or not, he did have a beach house to pay for. Not that he had it yet. But eventually, once there were a few million in the bank, he was going to leave this life behind and live in his million-dollar beach house with a dog that he didn't have yet either. Plus, looking at Ortiz' house, he definitely wasn't hurting for money.

Ortiz could tell by Thrower's face that his first offer was a little on the low side. "Or we could go for ten?"

Thrower lifted the corner of the left side of his lips, seemingly satisfied with that offer. And it was a good test at how well-off Ortiz really was. Anyone who just doubled their offer without even blinking was someone who had that to spare and then some. Truth be told, Thrower would work for free if it was someone in need. But Thrower did need a contribution to his beach house fund. And it was clear Ortiz had it to spare, and then some. It was a win for both parties.

"I take payment in advance," Thrower said.

"Of course. Of course. Eva, my dear. Will you please go inside and get my checkbook for me?"

Eva left, with her husband watching her every move as she gracefully walked around the pool.

"I take it her and the former missus don't get along well?" Thrower asked. "I assumed that was the chief hesitation in having your ex back."

Ortiz raised a brow and huffed. "Yes, it will be extremely awkward. Believe me, you will see. I was still married to Angelina when I met Eva. You can guess how things turned out from there."

"How long ago was that?"

"Eva and I met four years ago. Six months later, Angelina and I were divorced. It was… very messy. Then Eva and I got married a year after that. Do you have someone at home waiting for you?"

Thrower shook his head. "Not yet."

"You are better off that way, my friend. Life is a lot less complicated living like that."

"I'm sure."

Eva returned a few minutes later, checkbook in hand. She handed it to her husband, who immediately wrote a check, roughly equivalent to ten thousand United States dollars. He tore it out of the book and handed it to Thrower. Thrower briefly looked at it, then folded it in half and put it in his pocket.

"I assume you will be staying here?"

"I guess I could if you have room," Thrower replied.

"Oh, I have several guest rooms available. You can take your pick."

"I'll have to go back to my hotel and check out. Then I'll come back."

"Of course, of course. Whatever you need."

"Then we'll have to sit down and start going over a schedule."

"A schedule?"

"Do you plan on staying here for the next several weeks?" Thrower asked.

"Well, I do have a job that I need to attend to."

"Exactly. Like I said earlier, I can't be in two places at once. So in the instances where you're away from your family, we'll have to decide who I cling to."

"I'll go along with whatever you decide," Ortiz said.

"These other two guards, are they good? Do you trust them? How long have you known them?"

"I've known them about six months."

Thrower raised a brow. That wasn't much time. "That's it?"

"I started hiring when I got the other threats and decided to keep them on."

"Have they faced any action before?"

"Not to my knowledge. Definitely not while with me. I believe they spent some time in the army, though."

Thrower made a face. That didn't mean anything to him. He preferred being around people who'd actually been in the heat of battle before. There wasn't much he could do about it, though. It was who he had to work with.

"In any case, whoever I stick with in that particular instance, these other guys will need to stay with whoever I'm not with. I don't see any other way. Unless you decide to work from home until this situation is resolved."

"I have several important meetings coming up in the next several weeks. There are people flying in from several different countries to attend these meetings. I must attend them as well."

"OK," Thrower said. "But in the effort of making things easier for me, I'd really encourage you to stay home and work here as much as possible."

"I will do what I can. My family and I are in your hands."

Thrower stood up, with the others doing the same. He stuck his hand out and shook Ortiz' hand. "All right, then. Looks like you got yourself a bodyguard."

3

After checking out of his hotel room, Thrower's first order of business was going to the bank. It wasn't that he distrusted Ortiz in particular, but he wouldn't have been the first person to give him a phony check. Thrower had learned that lesson the hard way. Now, he asked for payment up front. And he made sure that payment was legit. Unless it was one of those cases where the money was negligible, or he didn't care about it. But in those instances where the money was supposed to be there, he made damn sure it was.

Once he found out the check was good, Thrower went back to Ortiz' house. Because of the nature of the job, he usually packed light. Ortiz was waiting for him once Thrower got there. He had a drink in his hand.

"You came back quickly. No trouble finding the place again?"

"This place isn't exactly hard to miss," Thrower replied.

Ortiz smiled. "Very true. Let me show you around."

Ortiz led Thrower around the house, giving him the fifty-cent tour. He showed Thrower every room in the house, outside, and around the perimeter of the property. He also introduced him to the two other guards. They both seemed competent at first glance. At least as much as one could deduce from a few minutes of conversation with each of them. But they seemed like they had their heads on their shoulders, they seemed to know what to expect, and they didn't appear to have any illusions about the job.

That was one of the things people outside of the profession usually got wrong. Some people assumed bodyguards saw a lot of action, in more ways than one. They thought bodyguards got into a lot of conflicts, the job was super interesting, and there were more women than you could shake a stick at.

But in reality, the job was rarely any of those things, and in most cases, it was none. More often than not, the job was slow, boring, the women were more interested in who he was protecting, and the days were long.

Except in Thrower's case. He seemed to be involved in the more interesting cases. Getting involved when the stakes were higher or the odds were riskier, is what made him the best of the best. Where some shrank and slivered away, and some just didn't want any part of it, Thrower rose up to the challenge. It was what made him who he was. And it was why he had the reputation that he did.

He wasn't yet sure about this case. He rarely had any preconceptions when he first got hired. He preferred to let things come to him. He watched, he observed, and then he acted. Of course, sometimes he was hired when the heat had already been turned up. Then he had no choice but to jump right in.

He didn't yet have a feeling which way this case would go. But he had a feeling about it. He wasn't sure what it was yet. But something was nagging at him that there was more than met the eye here. Of course, it could have just been his years of experience, telling him that things usually happened when he was around. But something was telling him this wouldn't be a boring assignment. He hoped he was wrong. But he rarely was.

Thrower and Ortiz continued talking, eventually winding up out back again, by the pool. Eva was in there swimming. Thrower looked around, noticing that Espinoza was no longer there.

"Where's Carlos?"

"Oh, he went home," Ortiz said. "Don't worry. If you're thinking he may be in danger too, I don't think so."

"Why not? Isn't he connected to you too?"

"Yes, but I doubt anyone would try to hurt me by hurting my assistant."

Thrower turned his head to the side, not as sure about that as his client was. "I've seen worse things happen to lesser people."

Ortiz tapped his new bodyguard on the back. "Well, if something happens, then I guess we will have to move him in here with the rest of us, huh?" Ortiz laughed. "It's like a hotel. Just one big happy family, no?"

Thrower grinned. "Yeah. One big happy family. How long has he been with you, anyway?"

"Who? Carlos?"

"Yeah."

"Oh, many years now. Maybe ten? Maybe less. I don't know. It's been a long time."

"You trust him?"

They abruptly stopped. "What? You think maybe Carlos has something to do with these threats?"

"He wouldn't be the first person to threaten and blackmail his boss."

Ortiz put his hand up. He wouldn't even think of such a thing. "No. No. Preposterous. Carlos wouldn't do such a thing."

"You're sure of that?"

"Positive. Carlos would not do that to me."

"Well, I wish I could be so positive," Thrower said. "But I have to consider all the possibilities."

"Of course. I understand that. But I'm telling you... it's not Carlos. I'd stake my life on that."

"Before this is over, you just might have to. You'd be surprised at how many of these situations are actually orchestrated by friends or family."

"Really?"

Thrower nodded. "Probably at least half."

"Now that's interesting. Very interesting. But I'm telling you, you're wrong about Carlos. He would never do it."

"Luckily, I'm not as attached to anybody as much as you are."

Ortiz tapped Thrower on the back again. "That's why you get paid the big bucks, my friend."

They continued walking around the grounds, with Thrower trying to learn as much as he could about the situation, as well as all the players in it.

"Did you call your wife? Ex-wife?"

Ortiz chuckled. "Not yet, my friend. I will do it in the morning. She is much more agreeable to things earlier in the day. Late afternoon, evening, forget about it. She is a bear. Even if I told her she had won a trip to a tropical island, she would decline because I was the one offering it to her."

"I'm sure it can't be that bad."

Ortiz put his index finger in the air and started waving it around. "Oh, you just wait and see, my friend. You will see. You have not met her yet. You have not talked to her. You will see. I promise you, you will see."

Thrower doubted the woman was as bad as Ortiz was making her out to be, but they were now divorced. That usually explained a lot. Most people didn't divorce amicably. Thrower was sure that the bad blood Ortiz was describing was just because of that. Plus the fact that Ortiz was now married and living with the woman he had an affair with while he was married to Angelina. That was enough to make any ex-wife pissed off permanently.

Still, he was willing to let Ortiz contact his ex on his own timeline. As long as that timeline didn't extend for a few more days. Thrower wasn't interested in extending his services to multiple locations. It just couldn't be done. It was going to be hard enough with Ortiz going out and about and leaving his family at home. That was something else that Thrower had in mind.

"What do you think about beefing up your security team?" Thrower asked.

"What, more men?"

"Well, by my count, there's five people who need protecting. You've got two guards and me."

Ortiz balked at the request. "Ah, I don't know. I think we have enough right now. Plus, you are like having five additional men, is it not?"

"I wouldn't go that far."

"Your reputation makes you out to be something else. Almost legendary."

"I'm definitely not a legend. I just know my job and I'm good at it."

"Carlos did a lot of digging on you. Your reputation is incredible."

"That being said, I think some extra men would be useful," Thrower said. "Especially if this drags on for a few weeks or even longer. There's bound to be sometimes when you, your kids, your wife, or your ex are all in different places at once. I can only do so much."

"I know that. We'll have to make sure we keep those instances to a minimum, eh? Plus, as you can tell, I am financially well off. But if I just keep on hiring bodyguards, I shall go broke."

"Somehow I think you can afford it."

Ortiz smiled. "Probably so. Still, let's stick with a small team for now. If it proves to be insufficient, then we will talk about additional men. Fair enough?"

"Assuming we're both still around to talk about it."

Ortiz tapped Thrower on the arm. "And as far as I'm concerned, there are only four people who need protection. Angelina can be sent on her way without an escort, in my estimation."

Thrower tilted his head and made a face, as if he couldn't believe he'd make such a statement. "Really? She is the mother of your children, you know. You did once love her."

Ortiz raised his arms, apologetic for his comments.

"You're right, of course. I shouldn't say such things. It was a terrible thing to say. Of course she deserves protection as well. Forgive me. It was quite rude."

"That's OK. These types of things can be nerve-wracking for everyone involved. Pressure and tension is high. And before this is over, it's probably going to get higher."

Thrower and Ortiz stopped about halfway back to the pool. Eva had gotten out of the pool, and Ortiz couldn't pass up the opportunity to look at her slender body as she walked over to a lounge chair.

"A remarkable woman, don't you think?"

Thrower glanced at her, then looked back at Ortiz and shrugged. "Sure." He rarely ogled over women, and he certainly wasn't comfortable doing it in the presence of a woman's husband.

The more Thrower talked to him, the more he found Ortiz to be an outgoing, free-spirited type of guy. Which was neither good nor bad by itself. Thrower did think that from experience, those types of people tended to be a bit more of a challenge for him. They usually made his work harder instead of easier by not taking his advice more seriously, or by not appreciating the severity of whatever situation they were in. He had a feeling this was going to be one of those.

"Who knows?" Ortiz said with a laugh. "Maybe this will all wind up being a big waste of time."

"Always possible."

"Perhaps this whole Liberation thing is just a

bunch of young punks hoping someone will scare easy and give them a big, fat payday."

"Can't rule it out," Thrower said, though he wasn't optimistic that was the case.

Ortiz continued laughing. "Maybe this will just be one big vacation for you, huh?"

"That would be nice. But I wouldn't say it's likely."

4

Thrower woke up, sitting up in the strange bed. He tapped his phone, which was on the nightstand next to the bed. It was morning. He heard a raised voice, which didn't take long to identify. It was Ortiz'.

Not sure what was going on, Thrower jumped out of bed and took out his gun from the drawer of the nightstand. He exited his new room, which was located on the first floor of Ortiz' home, and started looking for his employer. It didn't take long to identify where he was. Thrower followed the screaming.

It eventually led him to the living room, where Thrower saw Ortiz pacing back and forth while talking on the phone. Thrower took a breath, knowing that he could relax for the moment. At least nobody had broken into the house and was trying to kill Ortiz right then and there, which was Thrower's first fear.

The Bodyguard

Ortiz was talking in Spanish, and very fast at times, so Thrower couldn't make out everything that was being said. Through his travels, Thrower often picked up bits and pieces of different languages, with Spanish being one of them. He knew some words, could say a few different phrases, and maybe could hold a very brief conversation with someone about the basics, such as the time, weather, or location of something. But this conversation that Ortiz was having went far beyond what he could comprehend.

Whatever it was, it didn't sound pleasant. Ortiz seemed to be angry, raising his voice often, and his face kept turning different shades of red. Whoever he was speaking to, it didn't seem to be a friend. And after getting six hours of sleep, which was an average amount for Thrower, going back to bed didn't seem to be an option. Besides, Ortiz looked as if he was already dressed for work, having business clothes on, except for the jacket. Thrower figured he'd be on the move soon enough anyway.

Thrower put his gun inside the waistband of his pants, then leaned up against the wall as he waited for Ortiz to finish his conversation. Ortiz didn't seem to notice him. Of course, in Ortiz' state, Thrower wasn't sure the guy would notice an elephant trampling through the place. Ortiz just kept pacing around the room, circling the couch, looking down at the floor the entire time.

Eva then walked into the room, looking like she

was already dressed for pool time. She had a red bikini on, with a sheer coverup overtop that basically seemed useless for covering anything. She and Thrower locked eyes, with Thrower detecting the slightest hint of a devious smile as she walked past him.

Thrower didn't consider himself much of a ladies' man, but if there was one thing he was, it was observant. In his line of work, you had to learn how to read body language and facial expressions. Both things were important in assessing whatever type of situation you were in.

And he was sure that Eva was giving him the slightly seductive look of a woman who was expressing her interest without going overboard about it. Thrower watched her as she walked out of the room. She was a beautiful woman, no doubt about it. He could see what attracted Ortiz to her. As she left the room, she looked back at Thrower again, giving him another glimpse of that seductive grin on her face.

That could be problematic, he thought. He didn't usually like mixing business with pleasure, though he couldn't say he'd never done it. He also didn't like mixing things up with a married woman, especially one whose husband Thrower had been hired to protect. Messing around with a client's wife could get messy. Very messy. Those were situations Thrower tried to avoid. The job was tough enough without creating additional drama.

It wouldn't be much of a problem on his end.

Thrower had morals and willpower. He didn't need to covet her. But he'd also seen his share of women who threw themselves on top of any man who got near them. Of course, the same could be said for men who did the same to the opposite sex. Sometimes, saying no didn't always work. Especially when working in close proximity for a long period of time.

Thrower just had to hope that Eva wasn't one of those women who persisted, believing she could get anything she wanted. That would make the entire situation a whole lot more complicated. Way more complicated than it needed to be. Or should be. But that was a bridge he'd cross when and if he got to it. For now, he had to focus on Ortiz' problem. And judging by his phone call, he had a big one.

After about ten more minutes, with not much change in Ortiz' behavior while talking on the phone, he finally hung up. He angrily tossed the phone down on the couch as he passed it. He looked up and saw Thrower standing there.

"Do you believe that?" Ortiz said. If this had been a cartoon, there would have been steam coming out of his head. He was still heated. "Can you believe that? Can you believe the way she was talking to me?"

"Who?"

"Who? Angelina. My ex-wife. Remember I was supposed to call her today?"

"I remember," Thrower replied.

"Well, we talked."

Thrower faked a smile. "I assume that it didn't go well."

"Didn't go well?" Now Ortiz faked a laugh. "Didn't go well? That's the understatement of the year, my friend." He continued pacing around the couch. He finally stopped for a second and pointed at his bodyguard. "I told you, didn't I? I told you, she's a stubborn, vindictive woman who will argue about anything."

"She rejected your offer?"

"She doesn't even want to hear about it. She says my problems are my problems. Not to concern myself with her or the children. Can you believe that?"

"She's a woman scorned," Thrower said.

"She is a lunatic. She cannot be reasoned with."

"You're gonna call her back, right?"

Ortiz stopped pacing around and looked at him like he was crazy. "Call her back? Are you out of your mind? No, I am not going to call her back. I don't want anything to do with her. She is a crazy person. I do not have time in my life for that."

"Well, you can't just give up."

"Why not? I tried, and she doesn't want to hear it. What else can I do?"

"Try again?"

"Absolutely not," Ortiz replied. "I am done with her. Absolutely done with her."

"She's also the mother of your children. Don't you think you'd feel bad if something happened to her?"

"No."

Thrower gave him a look. He really didn't believe it. It was the anger talking.

Ortiz threw his arms up in frustration. "OK, OK, maybe I'd feel bad a little. But that's all. Just a little."

"And what about your kids?"

"What about them?"

"Don't they need to be protected?"

"Of course they do."

"Well, if they're with their mother and you want to protect them, then you gotta call her back."

Ortiz sighed and grunted, not wanting to call his ex-wife again. He wasn't sure he could take a second round with her already. He thought it over for a few seconds.

"Fine, fine, I will call her."

Ortiz picked up his phone from off the couch. He put it up to his ear without dialing the number. Thrower could tell he was stalling. Ortiz really didn't want to talk to her. It was almost comical.

After pacing around the couch two more times, Ortiz finally tossed the phone back down onto it.

"No. No. I can't do it. I can't."

"You can," Thrower said.

"You try it. See how you like it."

"I'm not saying it's fun. I'm not saying it's easy. But it's gotta be done."

Ortiz finally stopped walking around and plopped himself down on the couch. He put both hands on his face and rubbed it, the way someone does when they're exhausted. He felt like he'd already had a full day, and it was barely eight o'clock.

"That woman takes years off my life."

"If we don't bring her in, she might not have years," Thrower replied.

Ortiz looked at Thrower and shook his head. He knew what his bodyguard was telling him was true. He knew it was probably the right thing. But he had a hard time putting it into words.

"I have to go to the office soon. I don't have time for this. I don't have time for games with that woman."

Thrower could see how difficult it was for Ortiz. The whole situation seemed messy. He didn't really care about any of what had happened before with the marital problems. Thrower only cared about protecting whoever needed it now. In that vein, he tried to make it easier for his new client.

"I tell you what. Why don't we go to the office, you do what you gotta do, and on the way back here, we stop at Angelina's house?"

Ortiz once again gave him a crazy look. "Are you out of your mind?"

"What's wrong with that plan?"

"After the hard time she just gave me, you want me to show up at her house?" Ortiz started laughing. "Unannounced?"

"Is that a problem?"

Ortiz continued laughing. "No, that's not a problem. That's suicide. And you know what else? You won't need to worry about anything anymore after that. You won't need to be anyone's bodyguard. You know why? Because she will kill me herself. That's why. I just show up at her house, she will slap my face so hard, you will think an earthquake just hit the city."

"You just get us there. I'll do the talking."

Ortiz couldn't help himself. All he could do was laugh. "You've got balls of steel, my friend. You have no idea what you're up against."

That was true. But Thrower figured it couldn't be as bad as Ortiz was making it out to be. He thought Ortiz' problem was mostly because of what had happened before. And even if Angelina did turn out to be worse than Thrower was imagining, he could be persuasive. She wouldn't have been the first person he had to convince to get protection. And he was sure she wouldn't be the last. Thrower knew what buttons to push, regardless of the situation.

"I think I'll be able to handle it," Thrower said.

Ortiz just shook his head. "Maybe I should be protecting you, eh? Maybe I'll be attending your funeral, huh?"

Thrower smiled. "Maybe."

"I don't believe it can be done. She is a stubborn, stubborn woman. There is nothing you can say that will get her back in this house. Nothing."

"Sure of that, are you?"

"Yes. Nothing."

Thrower grinned. "I think there is."

Ortiz still shook his head, not believing it for a second. "I will make a wager with you."

"Name it."

"If you get her to accept our offer to come back here, I will pay you an extra thousand dollars per week. And if she does not, you take a thousand dollars less per week. What do you say?"

Thrower couldn't erase the smile from his face. This would be the easiest thousand dollars he ever made. "Deal."

"I wish you luck, my friend. You will need it."

"I'll be fine."

"If you convince Angelina to come back here, they shouldn't call you the Bodyguard. They should call you the Miracle Worker. Because that's what you will be. A miracle worker."

The Miracle Worker. Thrower thought about it for a moment. It had a nice ring to it. But it didn't sound as catchy as the Bodyguard in his mind. He instantly started thinking about how he was going to get Angelina to agree to come back. The extra thousand dollars in his pocket sounded nice, but he was more interested in making sure she and her kids were safe. That was the most important thing.

One thing Thrower did know was that he was getting her to come. One way or another. She was coming.

5

Thrower stood either next to or behind Ortiz most of the day. No matter where Ortiz went—though he was confined to his office building—Thrower followed. Even in the bathroom, Thrower stood guard outside. Nobody was getting to Ortiz while Thrower was around. At least, that was Thrower's way of thinking.

Ortiz appreciated Thrower's commitment to his job, while also not being uncomfortably close. While the bodyguard was nearby at all times, Thrower wasn't hovering over him or breathing down his neck. He did have a little bit of space. He was just never alone. Even in his office just signing papers or having a phone call, Thrower looked on.

Throughout the day, while making sure that Ortiz was protected, Thrower also kept his eyes open, analyzing everyone who even came somewhat near his client. Thrower watched for signs. Bad body language, a facial expression, someone who didn't appear all that happy when Ortiz was around, something to indicate that whoever had been threatening him was someone who was working for him. And there were several hundred of those.

But nothing jumped out at Thrower that sounded his alarm. Nobody gave him bad vibes or made him look twice. Everything seemed like a nice, ordinary day. Which was the way he liked it.

Ortiz was finishing up a meeting with eight other managers and supervisors. They were sitting at a long oval table, with Ortiz at the head of it. Thrower sat in the corner of the room, just over the left shoulder of Ortiz. It gave him a good vantage point, along with seeing anyone who might barge into the room.

Ortiz never bothered to introduce Thrower to anyone, and no one bothered to ask, just accepting his presence like it was no big deal. That only meant one thing to Thrower: Ortiz was a very powerful man. The fact that a stranger to them could be in the same room, listening to company secrets, and nobody batted an eyelash or asked who he was. It told Thrower that Ortiz could do what he wanted with very little pushback. Of course, it was his company, but even those in charge sometimes needed people who disagreed, or offered differing opinions, or just asked questions. But there didn't seem to be any in this lot.

The Bodyguard

The meeting went on for about an hour, with Thrower mostly bored by it. Nobody said anything interesting, and he really didn't even understand much of it. Most of it sounded like corporate-talk, which of course it was. These were the types of situations that made Thrower glad he chose the profession he did. Sure, his profession was more dangerous, and there were a lot of unknowns from day-to-day, but it sure was a lot more interesting. In just about every way.

Once the meeting had finally ended, Ortiz and his managers said their farewells to each other. Thrower stood back up, ready for the next part of their journey. Before the meeting started, Ortiz said this would be it for the day. That meant they only had one more stop before going back to Ortiz' place. Angelina's house. Thrower was sure that Ortiz would try to get out of it, or even pretend to forget about it altogether. But he didn't.

Ortiz was putting some papers in his briefcase and looked over at his bodyguard. "Well, are you ready to go, my friend?"

"In more ways than one."

Ortiz laughed. "Not as action-packed as you usually like it, I assume?"

"Not in the least."

Ortiz kept laughing, tapping Thrower on the arm. "Probably what makes you one of the best, huh?"

Thrower smiled. "Maybe. Can I ask you a question?"

"Anything. Ask away."

"You didn't explain me being here. And not one of the other people in here asked about me. Everybody just went along like it's business as usual."

"Because it is. Introductions are not necessary. Since you were behind me, they assumed you were with me, and since I brought you in, they know not to question it. They know that if I wanted them to know who you were, I would tell them. Since I didn't mention it, they know not to ask."

Thrower nodded. "Makes sense."

"I prefer not to publicize needing a bodyguard as much as possible. Bad for the image, you know?"

"I guess so."

"Plus, nobody else in the building knows about the threats other than Carlos. I'd rather keep it that way."

"Fine by me."

"Maybe after this is over, I'll have a position for you. Some executive manager type. What do you think?"

"I think I'd rather cut my fingers off," Thrower said.

Ortiz laughed a little harder than before. "You are not the business type."

"Not in the least. Meetings in offices and boardrooms aren't exactly my idea of a good time."

"Probably just as well, my friend. Your talents are needed elsewhere."

"Speaking of elsewhere, we have somewhere else we need to be."

Ortiz nodded. "Yes, I agree. I told Eva to prepare something extra nice for tonight. Wait until you get a taste of her cooking. She is a fabulous cook. You will see."

"That sounds very nice. But dinner isn't quite what I'm talking about."

Ortiz feigned ignorance, appearing to wrack his brain, trying to think of what Thrower was talking about. "Let's see, I came to work, had my meeting, dinner, Eva, I can't remember anything else?"

Thrower was positive Ortiz knew exactly what he was talking about. Nobody could be that forgetful or stupid.

"I'm pretty sure you know what I'm talking about. Your ex-wife? Remember her?"

Ortiz looked pained. "Ugh. You had to bring her up, didn't you? Why would you have to go and ruin a perfect day by bringing her into the conversation?"

"Because the conversation still needs to happen."

"Must we?"

"Your children, Manuel. Do it for your children."

"If only I was one of those fathers who didn't love their kids." Realizing what he'd said, Ortiz waved his hand in the air, as if he was erasing it from memory. "Forget I said it."

"We still need to get her into the fold."

Ortiz sighed, but capitulated. He pulled out his phone and sat back down. Figuring the conversation might take a while, Thrower took a seat around the table as well. It didn't take as long as Thrower thought it would, though. And it seemed to pick up right where it left off from the morning. Ortiz' face quickly turned red from anger, and his voice picked up steam quickly after that.

Thrower caught a word here and there, but he didn't need to understand anything to know how the conversation was going. Ortiz' body language told him everything. Besides looking exhausted, Ortiz kept sighing, shaking his head, raising his voice, and putting his hand on his head in frustration.

At some point, about five minutes into the conversation, it appeared that Ortiz had given up. He stopped talking, whether that was because he couldn't get a word in, or because he just figured it was a waste of time, Thrower wasn't sure. It honestly could've been both.

Not long after that, Ortiz slammed the phone down on the table. He still looked angry, though he wasn't verbalizing anything yet. He just had his hand over his mouth, shaking his head. Thrower didn't think it was necessary to ask how things went. Once the anger started fading from Ortiz' system, he glanced over at Thrower.

"You see? You see what she does? That woman!"

"Still won't agree, huh?" Thrower asked.

"I told her I have a problem, and I need her and the kids to stay with me for a couple of weeks, just to make sure everyone is safe and protected. You know what she said?"

Thrower shook his head. "Nope."

"She said she would rather be dead than stay with me for one day. She said whatever problem I have, I deserve it. She said it is karma for what I did to her. Can you believe that?"

"Uh, yeah, pretty sure I can."

"Forget her," Ortiz said. "I tried my best, right? I tried. I did what I could. If she doesn't want to come, I can't force her, right?"

"Right."

"Good. I'm glad you see it my way. So now we'll go home, right?"

"Wrong."

"Wrong? What do you mean, wrong?"

"We still need to bring her in," Thrower replied.

"What? You are crazy, my friend. Did you not just hear the conversation I had with her?"

"I heard it."

"And you heard me talk to her this morning?"

"Sure did."

"What else can I do?" Ortiz asked. "I can't pick her up and force her to come. She'd accuse me of kidnapping, I'm sure."

"I told you I'd talk to her. I'm sure I can get her to listen to reason."

Ortiz began laughing again. "Listen to reason? You are dreaming. You do not know this woman. She hasn't listened to reason since before we were married, let alone since then."

"Well, I'll take a crack at it, anyway."

"I hope you brought your bulletproof vest and your riot gear with you. You might need them."

From the way Ortiz described his ex, Thrower half-expected Angelina to be some female wrestler or some big-boned woman who was capable of tossing him around the room a few dozen times. He wasn't sure how much of that was real, and how much was just Ortiz overexaggerating things based on his relationship with her. Thrower would find out soon enough, though.

"Ready to get this over with?" Thrower asked.

"Am I ready? You're the one with the death wish, my friend. Are you ready?"

"No time like the present."

Thrower and Ortiz left the office and proceeded to walk to the elevator to leave the five-story building. Once they reached the lobby, Ortiz had someone get his driver to bring his car around to the front of the building. They stood there for a few minutes, with Ortiz still complaining about his ex-wife. Thrower was listening, but was still focused on his job, keeping his eyes open, watching everything.

At some point, Thrower started tuning Ortiz out. Not that he wasn't interested in what the man had to say, though it was getting repetitive, but his eyes caught a white van pulling into the parking lot. It seemed out

The Bodyguard

of place with the rest of the vehicles that were around. Most of the parked cars were newer, nicer looking, and mostly expensive.

This van had seen better days. It looked like a vehicle you'd put on a poster, warning people to avoid it at all costs. There were no hubcaps on the tires, the van was as dirty as could be, and it was moving slowly. They were all red flags for Thrower.

Ready to move quickly, Thrower put his hand on the back of Ortiz' shoulder, though he didn't want to alarm him unnecessarily yet. He wanted to be sure. But he didn't want to wait too long and have one or both of them dead.

Thrower looked around, figuring out where they could go for cover if the van suddenly made a beeline for them. He still kept the van in his peripheral vision, though. He turned around to see how far they were from the entrance of the building. They might be able to make it, though they had wandered a little ways away from it. They would be out in the open if they tried to duck back inside. That wasn't an appealing proposition. There were a few other cars that Thrower figured they could get behind if anyone in the van started shooting.

Of course, that only mattered if there were gunshots. It was also entirely possible that it could have been a kidnapping attempt. Or just a bid to rough Ortiz over. In those cases, Thrower had to prepare himself for a fight. That usually wasn't a problem, though. He was always ready.

Thrower put his eyes back on the van as it continued to creep closer to them. Now it was time to warn Ortiz. He needed to make sure that his client didn't panic. That never turned out well for anyone. Calm and steady usually won the race in these moments.

"If I say go, I want you to run over to that red car over there." Thrower nodded over to the car he was referring to. He didn't want to point and potentially tip off the van.

"What?"

"The red car to your right. If I say go, you get to that, and you get down and stay down."

"What's going on?" Ortiz asked.

"Don't worry about it. And don't panic. Stay calm. Trust me."

A sudden look of terror swept over Ortiz' face, unsure of what was happening. But he trusted his bodyguard and was willing to do whatever he told him was necessary.

"OK."

Thrower glanced over at the van, which started speeding up by now. That was alarming. The window on the passenger side began to roll down.

"Go!" Thrower yelled, knowing full well what came next. Windows rolling down only meant one thing. And it wasn't to shout insults.

The Bodyguard

Ortiz started to run, though Thrower gave him an extra push to get him going. As they ran, a gun pointed out the window of the van, taking aim at Ortiz. Now they had to rush their shot. The first bullet whizzed by Thrower and Ortiz, not appearing to hit anything of consequence. Another shot quickly rang out after that. It went past its target, shattering a back window of a car behind Thrower and Ortiz. Once they reached the red car, Thrower and Ortiz ducked behind it.

"What do we do now?"

"You stay put," Thrower said.

He then poked his head up over the car to see where the van was going. He was a little surprised, though, when the van's tires screeched as it came to a sudden halt. Usually in situations like this, the attacker took the shot, and kept on going, whether they were successful or not. The element of surprise was what they were going for. Once that was lost, they usually waited for another day. That was obviously not the case here.

Since the van was stopping, Thrower decided he was going on the offensive. He wasn't waiting for the fight to come to him. He was obviously an unknown to whoever they were. They wouldn't be expecting him to come at them. That gave him the advantage here. Next time, they might be ready. But for now, he had to take the advantage when he could get it.

Of course, the one issue he faced was that he didn't know how many men he'd be going up against. If it was one or two, he would have been able to handle that easily enough. More than that and it could get dicey. If it was more than two, he'd just have to make sure he roughed up the first couple enough to make the rest of them uneasy about tangling with him. That was the best he could hope for.

Thrower poked his head up to get a glimpse of the van as the door swung open. At the same time, he pushed Ortiz' head down even further. Thrower saw one man jump out of the passenger side of the van. He kept his eyes on him as the man ran towards the red car. As Thrower waited, he also noticed the back door to the van open as well.

Before the fight started, Thrower crouched down and moved to the back of the car, waiting for his opponent to get there. Fortunately, the stranger wasn't trying to be quiet. Thrower could hear the man running, getting closer. He wanted to time it just right.

Thrower jumped up from his crouched position, just as the man showed himself, anticipating his arrival perfectly. Thrower clotheslined the guy, who was several inches shorter and probably a few dozen pounds less than the well-built Thrower. The man easily went down, hitting the back of his head on the ground. Thrower kept up the pressure, though, not wanting to let the man back into the fight. He picked the man up, grabbed him by his clothes, and launched him over the trunk of the car.

Just as Thrower let go of the man, another person

The Bodyguard

appeared. This was the guy who came out of the back of the van. Thrower lost the element of surprise on this one. It didn't matter, though. He was no match for Thrower's fighting prowess. He tried to throw a couple of punches, but Thrower blocked them easily. Thrower returned the favor with a few shots of his own, nailing the man with a right, left, then another right. The last punch sent the man sprawling to the ground.

Thrower bent over to pick him up, but the man managed to squirm himself away, slithering backwards to get out of Thrower's reach. Thrower took a quick look around to brace himself for another challenger, but no one came. He then looked at the van again, staring directly at the driver, who was locking eyes with him as well.

The stare down lasted a few seconds as the driver wanted no part of whatever was going on. He was just waiting for his friends to get back into the van, which they did moments later. The men wanted no further part of tangling with Thrower. As soon as the men got back into the vehicle, the driver took off, with the van getting out of there as quickly as possible.

Thrower watched as the van left the premises, staring at it to ingrain the vehicle into his memory, just in case he ever crossed paths with it again. He tried to get a license number from it, but he didn't see one. He assumed they took it off before they got there.

He then looked down at Ortiz to make sure he was OK. Ortiz had his legs up to his chest, and buried his head into his arms, which were crossed over his knees. Thrower wasn't sure if he was praying, scared, or both. Not that it mattered much. Everything was over now. At least this incident. Thrower was sure there'd be others. He was very confident in that prediction. Whoever those people were, they would try again.

6

Thrower helped Ortiz get back to his feet. Ortiz brushed himself off, then looked around to make sure they were in the clear. He patted Thrower on the back.

"Thank you, my friend. You are worth your weight in gold already."

It was nice to hear his services were appreciated. But it was a little premature for congratulations just yet. They were just getting started. There was a long road ahead of them.

Thrower kept looking around. Something was gnawing at him. "Thanks. But there's some questions we need to find out the answers to."

"Such as?"

"For one, where's your car?"

Ortiz spun around to look for it. It wasn't in sight. "That's a good question."

"I got more. Second, they hit the moment we walked out of that building. How did they know you were leaving now?"

Ortiz looked confused, obviously not having any answers. "Another good question. So how did they?"

"Someone must have tipped them off."

Ortiz shrugged. "But who?" He then pointed back to his building. "You're not saying one of my people in there tipped them off, are you?"

"It makes sense, doesn't it?"

"No. No, I can't believe it."

"You can. You just won't. It doesn't have to be one of them inside, though."

"What do you mean? Who else would it be?"

"Well, your car's not here, and your driver's not here." Thrower hesitated for emphasis. "Put two and two together."

Ortiz put his thumb and index finger on his lips as he thought about it. "Juan."

"How long's he been with you?"

"Two or three years. I can't believe he would do such a thing."

"Any problems with him lately? Showing up late? Not being where he's supposed to be? Wanting a raise that you denied? Anything like that?"

Ortiz shook his head. "No. Juan has always been reliable and dependable. That's why I hired him and he's still here. If not, I would have gotten rid of him."

"Doesn't change the fact that neither he, nor the car, are here."

Ortiz tapped Thrower on the arm, wanting to get to the bottom of this. "Come. The car is parked behind the building. Let's take a look."

They walked briskly around the building to see what was going on with Ortiz' car. Along the way, Thrower thought of all the possibilities surrounding what had just happened. It didn't necessarily mean that Ortiz' driver was in on it or set him up. It was possible that the attackers had someone back there, watching and waiting, and when they saw Juan begin to bring the car up, they then alerted the people in the van to make their move. Of course, that didn't explain why Juan was gone.

But there were also other explanations. Maybe Juan had been paid off. When he got word that Ortiz was on the way out, he told the people in the van, then Juan took off. But there was also one other possibility that ran through Thrower's mind. Perhaps Juan was dead. Or at least, seriously injured. That would explain everything.

Thrower didn't think they would find Juan dead, though. Maybe it was more hope talking than actually feeling it. But they would find out soon enough. A lot more questions ran through Thrower's mind as they walked to find out Juan's fate. Like, why did the attackers initially shoot, then stop like they were attempting a kidnapping? Were they not trying to kill them at first? Were they just trying to scare them in an attempt to make the kidnapping easier, hoping that would make them less likely to resist? Did they suddenly change tactics right in the middle of things?

There were a lot of things going on here, and some of it didn't make sense yet. Thrower hoped they would get some answers soon. They finally got around the building, and Ortiz immediately pointed to his car. It was parked in its usual spot, alone, away from the other cars.

"I don't get it," Ortiz said. "Where's Juan?"

They didn't see the driver anywhere. Thrower knew from experience that bodies weren't always out where you could see them. He hoped it wasn't the case, but bodies had been known to be stuffed in a trunk or a back seat. Or just killed while they sat behind the wheel.

As they got closer to the black car, Thrower could see that nobody was in the front seat. Not unless they were on their side. Before they got too close, Thrower put his arm out to prevent Ortiz from going closer.

"Let me check things out first," Thrower said.

He wanted to make sure there wasn't someone hiding inside or behind the car. Once Thrower got to the driver's side window, he peeked inside, observing that it was empty. He walked around the entire vehicle, just to make sure nobody was there with a gun, waiting for them.

Thrower looked at Ortiz and waved him over.

Thrower kept glancing around, making sure there wasn't another car waiting to surprise them. Thankfully everything was quiet. Now, Thrower went to the trunk. He stood in front of it, wondering if there would be something inside. He pointed to it.

"Open it."

Ortiz threw his hands out to his side. "Why? What do you expect to find?"

"Hopefully nothing."

That was the truth. Thrower hoped he'd find an empty trunk. But it wouldn't be the first dead body he'd found in a trunk. He took out his gun and pointed it at the trunk. Though he hadn't experienced it personally, he had heard of stories of people waiting in trunks, surprising and killing the people who opened them. Those were obviously extreme cases. But this did appear like an extreme time. And Thrower wasn't going to be surprised.

Ortiz reached inside the car and pushed the button for the trunk to open. It was one of those trunks that opened automatically, without the need for someone to actually push it up. That worked in Thrower's favor, as he could stand off to the side of it. If someone was inside, they'd probably be assuming someone was standing right in front of them.

As the trunk opened, Thrower caught a glimpse inside. He was ready to throw down if need be. Luckily, it wouldn't be necessary. Thrower was happy to see that it was empty.

It did confirm one of his theories, though. It meant that Juan was somehow involved. Otherwise, he'd still be there. The fact that he wasn't dead, injured, or hiding in a back seat meant that he knew what was going on. Plus, Thrower was thankful the man wasn't dead. He hated finding dead bodies. It was easier to accept that someone was involved than to think they were an innocent casualty who left behind other innocent people who would be impacted by their death.

Once Ortiz saw Thrower put his gun away, he went back to the trunk and looked inside.

"There's nothing there."

"I know," Thrower said.

"What were you looking for?"

"Juan."

"Oh, you thought maybe they had tied him up and put him in there?"

"Something like that."

Ortiz looked around again, hoping to see his driver somewhere. Even if he was just walking around. "I don't get it. Where is Juan?"

"Already told you. He's probably gone."

"Gone? Gone where?"

"Depends on how involved he is," Thrower replied. "If he's one of the people who's planned this thing, then he's probably helping to plan their next move. If he's just a guy who got some money to look the other way here, then he's probably on the next plane out of here."

Ortiz sighed. "I still can't believe it. I still can't believe it. He's been with me for three years. Why would he do such a thing? Why would he be mixed up with these people?"

"Money talks."

"How much could they have given him?"

Thrower shrugged. "I don't know. Obviously more than you were paying him."

Ortiz put his hands on top of his head, still having a hard time accepting it. "I just... I don't understand. Why?"

"Does Juan have family here?"

"I don't know."

Thrower looked at him strangely. "You've got a driver who's worked for you for three years and you don't know if he's got family?"

Ortiz looked at a loss for words. "Uh, well, you know... things happen and... some things don't come up."

"What about his address?"

"His address?"

Thrower sighed. He already knew what this answer was going to be. "Yes, his address. You know, where he lives?"

"Oh, that. Yes, well, I'm, uh... not exactly sure."

"How can you not be sure where the guy lives?"

"Because I don't go and visit him where he lives," Ortiz said. "He works for me. He shows up to my house and my work and takes me where I need to go. Not the other way around."

Thrower shook his head. He figured it was more like a powerful and wealthy man who didn't care and didn't want to take the time to find out more about the people who worked for him.

"What difference does it make?"

"Because if he's got a wife and kids, he could be on his way there to pack them up," Thrower said. "We could possibly get to them first, then when Juan shows up, we grab him, make him tell us what he knows."

"Oh, very smart thinking."

"Not that it does us any good since we don't know where he lives."

"I am sorry," Ortiz said. "I know, perhaps, I am not the greatest boss. Maybe I don't know as much as I should. We are all human. We make mistakes."

Thrower agreed with that. "You're sure you haven't had any problems with him before? Maybe something you shrugged off or didn't think much about?"

Ortiz lowered his head, crossed his arms, and put his hand over his mouth as he thought about it. After a little time, he slowly shook his head.

"No. Nothing that I can think of. Sorry. Nothing comes to mind."

Thrower closed the trunk as he thought about their next steps. Those thoughts quickly turned to Ortiz' ex-wife and kids. Things had escalated now. Whether they were trying to kill Ortiz, or kidnap him, or just rough him up some, there was definitely an escalation. The group wasn't just sending letters and making threats. Now, they were carrying them out.

That meant that Angelina and the kids may be their next target. Especially if they thought they were vulnerable. Whatever their plan was here with Ortiz, it had failed. That may embolden them to take a run at his family. Thrower had to get there in time to stop it. Even if he was wrong and they weren't in danger at the moment, he'd rather assume the worst and get to them first than find out later that something had happened to them that could have been prevented.

"We gotta get to your wife and kids," Thrower said. "Now."

Ortiz could hear the urgency in Thrower's voice. "You think they will try to harm them now?"

"I don't know. But I don't wanna take chances. Do you?"

"No, you're right. We must go to them."

Thrower walked around to the passenger side of the car. "Since I don't know where they live, or the area, you're driving."

"You mean I have to drive myself?"

"No." Thrower smiled. "You're driving me."

"But I don't... drive myself."

"Well, you are today."

"Oh, dear."

Ortiz got behind the wheel, looking like he'd never

operated a vehicle before. Thrower gave him a weird look.

"You have driven before, right?"

"Yes, of course," Ortiz answered. "Many times. Though, it has been a while. I just need to get familiar with everything again."

"Let me help you out." Thrower started pointing to everything. "That's the wheel. You steer with it. Those pedals on the floor are for speeding up and braking. This thing here, that's for putting the car in drive, neutral, or reverse. And that's pretty much all there is to it."

"Yes, yes, of course."

Ortiz put the car in drive, sputtering a little at first. Thrower put his hand over his eyes, hoping they'd make it there in one piece. After a minute or so, they finally got out of the parking lot and headed straight for Angelina's place. If the attackers went straight there, Thrower and Ortiz had some time to make up. They just hoped they wouldn't be too late.

7

There were a few hairy moments on the drive over to Angelina's house, but they got there in one piece, and it didn't take that long. Somehow, Thrower was able to avoid covering his eyes on the way there.

Angelina lived in a nice house, with a gate at the front of it. That's why it was alarming when they got there and saw that the gate was open. Ortiz stopped the car before going through it.

"Uh-oh," Ortiz said.

"What? What's the matter?"

"The gate is open. She never leaves the gate open."

"Could she have just gotten home or something?"

Ortiz shook his head. "No. Never. She is very big on security. Especially where the children are concerned."

"Drive on through."

Ortiz put the car in motion again, driving through

the opened gate. It didn't take long before they saw what the problem was.

"Is that?"

"Hurry up and park," Thrower said.

There was a white van parked to the side of the house. The same white van that attacked them at Ortiz' business. Ortiz parked the car on the other side of the house.

"What do we do?" Ortiz asked.

"You stay here."

"But my kids?"

"You stay here," Thrower repeated, more forcefully this time. "And get down. I don't want these guys seeing you. If they come out in a hurry and see you and I'm not here, you might be in trouble."

"Shouldn't I go with you, then?"

"Definitely more trouble where I'm going. Just get down and out of sight."

Thrower jumped out of the car, with Ortiz sliding down onto the floor of the back seat. Thrower first jogged over to the van to see if there was anyone inside. Before he got there, he could see the arm of the driver sticking out the open window.

As Thrower approached the van, he tried to take an angle, that way the driver couldn't see him through the side mirror or turn his head and locate him. Thrower got there quickly, though, knowing the others might have been inside the house. Just as Thrower got to the window, he wanted to make sure the other guy had his head turned toward him.

"Hey!"

The man turned to look out the window, only to receive a thunderous left hand from Thrower. The man was knocked back, allowing Thrower to quickly open the door. Thrower put his hands on the man and dragged him out of the van. Thrower then started working him over, kneeing him in the stomach and taking his head and hitting the back of it repeatedly against the side of the vehicle. Once Thrower was done with that, he unleashed a few left and right hands, eventually dropping the man.

Thrower then turned toward the house, though he didn't get too far, as he heard a woman screaming. He knew one of the men was about to come out with Angelina. Thrower wanted to meet them at the door and catch them by surprise.

He raced over to the front of the house, getting there just in time. One of the men was pulling Angelina through the door, though she was trying her best to resist. The man was having a hard time with her, and his attention wasn't anywhere but the woman.

That allowed Thrower to get the jump on him. Thrower didn't want to hurt Angelina at the same time, so he first kicked at the man's legs, forcing him to release Angelina. Once that happened, and Angelina raced back inside for her children, Thrower went to work. He unleashed several shots to the man's midsection, causing him to hunch over in pain. Thrower then connected on an uppercut, sending him sprawling to the ground.

Thrower then rushed inside, hearing a commotion. He went to the right of the house, seeing Angelina trying to fight off the last stranger, who was trying to round up her two children. Now with Angelina in the middle of it, the man was trying to keep her at bay, which allowed the children to get away.

Now Thrower was in the middle of it, and he'd make sure it ended quickly. The man with Angelina saw Thrower coming and immediately let go of her, knowing what kind of fight he had on his hands. He recognized Thrower from their confrontation at Ortiz' business, though he was most familiar with Thrower's fists. The man was still hurting from their first encounter.

Both men got into a boxing position, balling their hands into fists and holding them out in front of their chests. Thrower definitely looked like a man more comfortable in that position than the other guy. Thrower's opponent didn't exactly look like he wanted to throw hands. He looked tentative and kept his distance. He was actually trying to get Thrower to move his feet and his position, that way he had a lane to the door to escape.

Thrower wasn't particularly interested in having this go on for too long and started moving closer. He knew the other two men outside were down, but they wouldn't stay that way forever. He wanted to get Ortiz' family to safety. That meant he had to end this fight quickly.

The other man tried to stall for as long as possible. He really had no interest in battling Thrower again. Thrower was bigger, looked meaner, and could obviously fight, which he knew from their last encounter.

Suddenly, there was a car horn blaring. Thrower looked over to the window. It sounded as if it was coming from where the van was parked. Then the horn blasted again, this time a little longer than the first time.

That was the man's cue, as he ran for the front door, hoping to squeeze by Thrower. There was a small lane to go for it, but Thrower probably could have cut the man off if he really wanted to. But if the man was looking to go, that meant the attackers weren't interested in continuing the fight. That was good enough for Thrower. He didn't want to keep it up against the three men any further either. If they wanted to get out of there, he wasn't going to stop them.

Once the man ran out the front door, Thrower went over to it as well. He stood there, watching as the last man jumped into the back of the van. As soon as the guy was in, the van sped off, going out through the front gate.

With the van gone, Thrower was finally able to breathe a sigh of relief. He turned around to find Angelina, though she wasn't initially in sight. A few seconds later, she appeared, with an arm around each of her children.

"You OK?" Thrower asked.

The woman was understandably upset after what had just happened. "Yes, thank God. Thank you so much for helping. I don't know how I can repay you."

"I'm just glad I was able to get here in time and could help."

Angelina's face went from shock to anger, as she now saw her ex-husband standing by the door. "What the hell are you doing here?"

Ortiz opened his arms wide. "What do you mean, what am I doing here? I'm here to make sure you're OK. Why else would I be here?"

"I don't know. You only ever come around when you want to try to swindle me or cheat me."

Ortiz rolled his eyes. "Oh, come on. I come here out of the goodness of my heart..."

"The goodness of your heart?" Angelina laughed. "That's a funny one. What heart? I didn't know you still had one."

"Here we go. Here we go. Now comes the insults."

"What else do you expect?"

"From you, nothing. That's exactly what I expect."

Thrower stood there, looking defeated as one does when things spiral out of control. He thought this conversation qualified. Conversation. More like the precursor to another war. Though he didn't want to, he let them argue it out for a few more minutes. He figured it was better if they just got it out of their systems, that way they didn't bottle it up inside to the point where he had to listen to it the rest of the day or the next few days. Maybe if they just said it all now, that would squash it for later.

Thrower had finally had enough. They started repeating themselves, and it didn't seem to be letting up. It actually looked like they could have kept this up the rest of the night. He wouldn't have been surprised if he left, came back the next day, only to find them in the same exact position, still arguing.

"Enough!" Thrower put his arms out towards each of the verbal combatants, letting them know it was time to quiet down. "That's it."

Ortiz didn't seem ready to stop, though. "She was the one who—"

Angelina didn't seem ready to let it go, either. "Oh, I'm the one who started this? Is that what you're saying?"

"Yes, that's what I'm saying!"

Thrower's shoulders slumped as the two continued their verbal assault on each other. He crossed his arms, letting it go on for another minute or two. They obviously weren't done. If this was what their marriage was like, he could see why it ended. Of course, maybe this was only the result of how it ended. Either way, he wasn't really interested in listening to it anymore.

"Enough!" Thrower yelled again. "That's it. No more. We're done." This time, he put his big frame in between the two of them, giving each of them a healthy and hopefully intimidating stare. "Right? We're done?"

Ortiz put his hands up, moving his arms and head all around. "Yeah, yeah, we're done. Or I'm done, at least."

That drew another round from his ex-wife. "Oh, you're done? So what you're saying is that I'm not?"

Ortiz threw his hands up high above his head for emphasis. "If that's what it seems like."

Angelina started to respond, but Thrower quickly put a stop to that. He turned toward her and put his index finger in the air to let her know he wasn't putting up with anything else.

"No more," he said quietly.

Angelina nodded, looking embarrassed by the whole incident.

Thrower continued, hoping to reason with both of them, if that was even possible. "With everything that just happened, nobody here should be fighting with anyone. We should all be thankful we're all fine, we're all healthy, nobody's hurt, and let's figure out where to go from here."

Angelina pointed to her ex-husband. "Well, I know where he can go from here. Out!"

"Oh, come on!" Ortiz replied. "I came here out of my concern for you, and this is the thanks I get?!"

"Your concern for me?! Ha! That's a joke."

"Oh really?"

"Yes, really!"

Thrower sighed, realizing this was likely going to take a little longer than he'd expected. He could try to stop it again, but it was clear they had quite a bit to say to each other. And none of it good. He went over to the window and looked out, making sure the white van hadn't come back, or there weren't some other unwelcome visitors lurking out there.

With it being clear outside, and without any immediate danger—at least from anyone outside—Thrower found himself a chair and plopped down in it. If there was popcorn available, he would've made himself a bowl and watched the entertainment. Instead, he just let the two of them battle it out, hoping they'd get it out of their systems soon enough. He looked out the window a few more times as the fight raged on. One thing was for sure: this was going to take a while.

8

Thrower sat there in a chair, his arms folded across his chest, as he watched and listened to the formerly married couple argue. Eventually, the argument died down. It took about twenty minutes, though. But just like Thrower had hoped, the two eventually seemed to get tired of arguing. Or maybe they said everything they had to say. In either case, the battle seemed to be over.

Both Ortiz and Angelina awkwardly stood there, looking at each other, as if they were each waiting for the other one to start up again. But they were both done. Unless one of them said something stupid to get the other one going.

"Are we good now?" Thrower asked.

Ortiz glanced over at him, almost like he'd forgotten he was there. "Oh. Yeah. Sorry." He looked at his ex-wife once more. "I'm done."

Angelina looked over at Thrower, too. "I'm done."

"Good," Thrower said, standing up. "Now, can we get on with what we're here for?"

"What are you here for? You didn't just happen to come by, did you?"

"No."

"He works for me," Ortiz said.

Angelina gave her former partner an evil glance before softening her eyes as she looked back at Thrower. "You knew this was going to happen?"

Thrower shook his head. "We didn't know. We came here just in case. There was some trouble elsewhere, and I thought it'd be a good idea to come here and check in on you."

"Thank you. What other trouble was there?"

Ortiz answered. "Coming out of the business, the same white van, with the same men, took some shots at me, then got out to try to either kill me or kidnap me."

Angelina folded her arms as she processed everything she was learning. "And why would they come here for me?"

"Well, they had a chance to kill you and didn't," Thrower replied. "That would make it seem like they were going to kidnap you and probably exchange you for a ransom."

Though she wasn't happy about it, and it was obviously upsetting, she seemed to be keeping a level head about it. "Who are these people?"

"I don't know yet."

"Who are you? I've never seen you before, and I've never heard Manuel mention you before."

"My name's Nate Thrower. Your husband hired me to protect him."

"Ex-husband."

"Sorry. Ex-husband."

"So you're a bodyguard?"

"He's not just *a* bodyguard," Ortiz said. "He is *the* bodyguard. He has a reputation for this sort of thing. He is one of the best."

Thrower tried to downplay the notion of him being some kind of superman. "I do have experience with these types of situations."

"If you're hiring a bodyguard, and these people are doing all these crazy sorts of things, why am I just hearing about it now? Did you know me and my children might be a target?"

Thrower gave her a strange look. He then turned toward Ortiz, getting the feeling someone wasn't getting all the information they should have. He had an idea who was who.

"Did he not call you this morning and tell you about all this?" Thrower asked.

"He called me, but he didn't mention any threats or anything."

Thrower sighed, then scowled at his client. "I told you to call her and tell her exactly what was going on, so she would know."

"Well, I did," Ortiz said, waving his arms out in front of him. "I did."

Thrower looked at each of them. "Well, something's getting lost in the translation here."

"I called and said I had some things to discuss, and..."

"And?"

"And she didn't let me finish. She does what she always does. She interrupts, she argues, she belittles me, and then I get frustrated to the point where I forget what I called for."

Angelina was about to say something in return, but Thrower quickly put a stop to that. He wasn't going to listen to them fighting for another half hour. He stepped in front of Ortiz, so Angelina could only focus on him and what he was saying.

"Look, there's obviously some kind of threat here," Thrower said. "I don't know who these people are or what their intentions are, though now we kind of have an idea. Everyone is in danger here. Including you and your children."

Angelina glanced over at her children, who were sitting on a couch. She was concerned for their safety more than anything. "Why are these people after us? We haven't done anything."

"Your husband... ex-husband, has obviously ticked someone off. Right now, everyone associated with him is in the line of fire. That includes you."

"What am I supposed to do?"

"I want to try to protect you and your kids, but I can't be in multiple places at once. I can't protect you here, and Manuel at work, and Eva at their house, it's just too much."

"What are you suggesting?"

"I'm suggesting that you and the kids go with us to Manuel's house for the next few weeks until this hopefully gets sorted out."

Angelina's eyes almost bulged out of her head. She'd never thought she'd get the offer to live back in that house again. "Are you kidding?"

A sly-looking grin formed on Thrower's lips. He knew what he was asking, and he knew why she would have trouble with it. Still, it was the only way. At least for the moment.

"I know it would be difficult."

"Difficult?" Angelina said. "Difficult? Try impossible. I can't go back to that house again. Not in a million years."

"It's the only way I can try to protect you."

"So I'll get police protection."

Ortiz started laughing. "Police protection. That's a good one."

"What's so funny?" Angelina asked.

"You know as well as I do what the situation is with the police down here. Maybe you get a good one, maybe you get one on the take. Maybe you get one who's involved in this thing."

Angelina grunted her unhappiness with the whole

situation. She kept shaking her head without saying another word.

"Listen, I've heard about the past," Thrower said. "I know it's not an ideal situation for you. But we're not dealing with an ideal situation. You've seen what can happen here if you're not protected and I'm not here. I wouldn't ask if I thought there was another way."

"You want me to go back and live in that house, under the same roof as that woman who slept with my husband behind my back, and then stole him away from me? That's what you're asking?"

Thrower nodded. "Yes, that's what I'm asking. Like I said, I don't know what other choice there is."

Angelina looked past Thrower at Ortiz, who was back within her view. "Why don't you hire a team of bodyguards to stand outside here twenty-four hours a day?"

"I've already hired the best," Ortiz answered, holding his arm out toward Thrower.

"Yeah, for you. What about us? Don't your children deserve some consideration?"

"From where? Where would you like me to hire these people? What if I hire someone and he's involved somehow? What then? The only person I know I can count on right now is standing right here."

"This is unbelievable. How could you be so selfish?"

"Me selfish? Am I not here to save you right now?"

"Really? You're saving me? I didn't see you lift a

finger to fight off these men. I didn't see you putting a guard on my door to help warn me before these people got here. What exactly are you saving me from?"

"Let's settle down," Thrower said, wanting to avoid a repeat from earlier. "Look, whatever should have been done that wasn't done—or could have been done—that's all in the past. We can't change that now. All we can do is change what we're doing from this moment forward. And that's getting you and your children to safety right now. If I leave here, I can't guarantee these men won't be back for you."

Angelina sighed loudly, still not thrilled with the situation. "And how long would we have to stay there?"

Thrower lifted his hands. "I don't know. I'm not going to lie to you and tell you it's only going to be a few days. I really don't know. We're playing defense here. It could be a few days, it could be a few weeks, or maybe even more than that. I'm asking you to trust me."

Angelina still wasn't happy, but considering the man did save them once already, she didn't see another choice at the moment. "You were here and saved us. That means something to me. I will trust you. I will agree to go. But I want to talk further about this."

Thrower nodded, willing to talk about anything as long as she agreed to go. "Fine. We can talk."

"I still think we should have extra protection. As you said, it's just you."

"I have a couple of other men," Ortiz said.

"I'm not talking to you about this," Angelina replied. "I'm talking to the expert."

"Let's just pack up your things, whatever you need for the kids, and we can talk about whatever you want once we're settled again."

Angelina still didn't look happy, but agreed it was for the best. She left the room and went into a bedroom to start packing. Thrower let out a sigh of relief and ran his hand over his head. He didn't know what was in store for any of them, but it was sure likely to be interesting.

9

Thrower and Ortiz were standing by the car, waiting for Angelina and the kids to come out of the house.

"This is going to be so awkward," Ortiz said. "Could it get any worse?"

"Sure it could," Thrower replied. "You could be dead."

Ortiz made a face, knowing that was true. But he never thought he'd see the day when Angelina moved back in with him.

"Hey, you did tell your wife that they were coming, right?"

Ortiz started shaking his body around, the way he did when he tried to avoid answering a question truthfully. "Well, I mean, she knows that they're coming. Maybe not today, but... she knows they are coming."

Thrower shook his head. "When are you going to

stop beating around the bush with people and just tell them what they need to know?"

"Hey, I am a work in progress, OK? I'm working on it."

"How's Eva with the kids?"

"Oh, she's fine. There are no problems there."

"The kids like her?" Thrower asked.

"Yes, as far as I know. She'll take them out shopping, to the park, plays in the yard with them, there are no problems there."

"And have Angelina and Eva been in the same room since all this happened?"

"Not technically in the same room," Ortiz answered. "They have seen each other; they have been outside in close contact with each other."

"Friendly?"

Ortiz laughed. "Friendly? I mean, I don't think they will get out the boxing gloves, but you probably won't hear many words spoken between them."

"Dirty looks, icy stares, and cold shoulders?"

Ortiz tapped Thrower on the shoulder. "You got it."

They waited about five more minutes before Angelina and the kids showed their faces again. The trunk was already open, and they put several suitcases inside. After closing the trunk, Angelina looked around.

"Where's your driver?"

"Oh, that is a long story," Ortiz replied.

"He quit?"

"Well, technically, I suppose."

"We think he might be mixed up with those people in the van," Thrower said.

"What?" Angelina said.

"Certainly looks that way."

Angelina turned towards her ex-husband. "What have you gotten yourself mixed up in?"

Ortiz pleaded ignorance. "I don't know. I don't know. I've done nothing. All I've done is the same I've ever done. I go to work, I do business, I come home, and that's it. That's it. I do not know why these people are targeting me."

"How long has this been going on?"

"I don't know. The threats come every now and then."

"For how long?"

"Months, a year, I don't know."

Angelina was surprised to hear it was that long. "You've been getting threats for a year, and you didn't think it was a good idea to let your family know so they could protect themselves? A year?"

"Maybe less."

Thrower could sense things were starting to get heated again and stepped in between them. "What's done is done. We can't change it. Let's just get in the car, we'll go back to the house, and we'll figure things out from there."

Ortiz went to the driver's side, drawing a laugh from his ex.

The Bodyguard

"You're driving?" Angelina's face indicated she could hardly believe it.

"Is that so difficult to believe?"

"Yes! In all the time we were together, I don't remember you ever driving once. You always had a driver. Someone to chauffeur you around."

"Well, I am a changed man now."

Angelina laughed again. "That's a good one."

Ortiz stood there with his mouth open, looking like he was contemplating firing back with some verbal jabs of his own. He was able to refrain, though. He had a little help, as Thrower nonchalantly put his hand up, telling Ortiz to not fight back. Thrower opened up the rear door, letting Angelina and the kids get in.

Once they were inside, Thrower went around to the passenger side and hopped in. Ortiz put the car in drive.

"Hope we don't crash on the way there," Angelina said.

"You know what?" Ortiz replied.

Thrower quickly got in the middle of it to put a stop to it. "Hey, I'm gonna tell both of you to knock it off right now. OK? I'm not dealing with it anymore. Stop the snide comments, stop the bickering, and let's try to work together to get through this. Then once this is over, and I'm gone, you can have at each other. But I'm not going to keep listening to it. Because if I do, I'm either gonna leave and let you deal with this on your own, or I'll just lock the two of you in separate closets so I don't have to deal with you at all."

"You're right," Angelina said. "I'm sorry. I will concentrate on the problem at hand from here on out."

"I agree, too," Ortiz said. "The bickering amongst each other solves nothing."

It was a quiet car ride for the next few minutes, which was soothing to Thrower's ears. It was a thirty-minute drive back to Ortiz' house, and Thrower could only hope it would remain a quiet and pleasant one. He wouldn't be able to take their bantering the entire way there.

The only thing Thrower was worried about was that they might see the white van again. Or a different car altogether. The attackers seemed to be aggressive, trying to hit two targets right after each other, and Thrower was concerned that the pattern may continue. If the attackers were amped up and pissed off about coming up empty two times, they might have been in a mood to continue until they got it right.

With that in mind, Thrower had his eyes open. He was constantly looking in the mirrors to see if he could spot anything that looked like it might be danger lurking. Luckily, there wasn't anything so far. But it was still a long trip back to Ortiz' house, and anything could happen along the way.

The only thing Thrower could hope for was that the attackers were disappointed about failing two times already and decided to regroup and think of a

The Bodyguard

new plan, which might take a few more days. It wouldn't take long, though, before he realized that wasn't happening. After being on the road for less than ten minutes, Thrower noticed a white van several cars behind them. It sure looked like the same van they'd come across two times already.

Thrower kept his eyes firmly planted in the mirror for the next several minutes. He didn't alert the others yet, not wanting to alarm them until he knew for sure that it was the same vehicle. After making a few more turns, the van continued to follow them. Thrower was sure that it was their attackers.

Thrower wasn't sure what the men in the van were planning, but he knew it wasn't good. He hoped Ortiz would be able to outmaneuver them if possible, though he wasn't sure how likely that was. He thought about telling Ortiz to pull over, allowing Thrower to get behind the wheel, since he had experience in these types of situations and would be more likely able to evade the van. But that would mean stopping. And stopping might have been what the attackers were hoping for.

They'd just have to go along with what they were doing and hope for the best. Thrower waited another minute before telling the others what he thought was happening.

"Looks like we've got company."

Ortiz immediately started twisting his head around. "What? Where?"

"Just keep your eyes on the road and drive back to the house," Thrower said. "I've got my eyes on them."

"Who?"

"Our friends in the van."

"They're back?"

"Sure looks like it." Thrower observed them in the mirror, though they were now only two cars away from them.

"What are they doing?"

"Don't know. I expect we'll find out soon enough."

Thrower looked into the back seat and saw Angelina holding her children tight. "Get down on the floor."

"Why?" Angelina asked.

"I don't know what they're planning, but if there's any shooting, the floor's the best place for you."

They immediately got down on the floor, with Angelina hovering over top of her kids to try to protect them as much as she could.

"Should I speed up?" Ortiz asked.

Thrower was calm, still looking in the mirror. "Just go your normal speed."

"But what if they attack?"

Thrower pulled out his gun, double checking the magazine that was in it. "Then we'll deal with it."

"Oh my god, who are these people?"

"Hey, did you recognize any of them when they were coming out of the house?"

"No, you told me to stay down."

"And you actually listened?" Thrower asked.

"Well, for the most part. I mean, I may have been peeking a little."

"Well, I'm not gonna spank you for not listening. Did you recognize any of them or not?"

"Oh. No. No, none of them looked familiar to me." Ortiz noticed Thrower making a face. "Is that good or bad?"

"Is what good or bad?"

"That I didn't recognize any of them."

"It's neither," Thrower replied. "If you recognized them, it would've made things easier to identify who's behind this. Doesn't really change anything at the moment, though."

After another minute or two, the car between them and the van turned, leaving no other vehicle between them. Thrower thought the van was beginning to speed up. That left no doubt in his mind. Something was about to go down. The van wasn't just following them for surveillance purposes, or trying to make them nervous. They were about to try something for the third time in a row.

"Gotta admire them for their persistence," Thrower said.

"What?" Ortiz asked.

"Nothing."

Ortiz kept looking in the rearview mirror. He could see the van was gaining ground on them. And he was getting nervous. "I think I should speed up."

Thrower shrugged. He seemed ambivalent about it. "If you want."

"Do you think that will get rid of them?"

Considering who was driving, Thrower thought that was unlikely. "I doubt it."

"What do you think they're up to?"

"I don't know," Thrower said. "But I think we're about to find out."

10

They continued driving toward Ortiz' house, even speeding up a little, though it didn't put any more distance between them and the van. The trailing vehicle was keeping up with them. Thrower was preparing himself for something to happen. The fact that the van wasn't trying to disguise themselves meant they were getting ready to do something. And soon.

If the van was just planning on surveillance—or something else that was non-violent—they probably would have hung back more. They would have tried to keep themselves hidden. But they didn't. They didn't seem to care that they were noticed. That was for a reason. Thrower figured it was because they were going to try to overwhelm them.

He wasn't wrong.

As soon as Ortiz turned a corner and the traffic lightened up a bit, the van finally made its move. It sped around to the side of the car, then forcefully slammed into it. Ortiz briefly lost control of the wheel, but somehow was able to get it back.

"I can't believe this!" Ortiz said.

Angelina and the kids started to scream, and the girl started to cry. Thrower remained calm, though. He held on and looked past Ortiz through the driver's side window to try to get a glimpse inside the van. Any small thing he could pick up at this point might be helpful for later.

The whole event only lasted a few seconds. After the two vehicles bumped together a few more times, the van finally was able to complete its objective. It slammed into the side of the car again, but this time Ortiz wasn't able to keep it under control. The car slid off the road and rammed into a side wall, eventually coming to a stop.

The van jammed on its brakes just ahead of where the car had finally stopped. Everyone was shaken, but no one was seriously injured. Thrower knew it was about to hit the fan. Once again, he wasn't playing defense. With his gun in hand, he tried to jump out of the car. He couldn't get the door open, though. His side of the car was jammed up against the wall, and he couldn't get out. That wasn't going to stop him, though.

"Everyone stay down," Thrower said.

He helped push Ortiz down to keep him out of sight. Thrower looked through the windshield and saw one of the men get out of the van. Thrower immediately opened up, firing several rounds at him.

The shots surprised the man, who instantly backed up, eventually getting back in the van. Thrower fired a couple more rounds, wanting to keep the pressure on. The man who jumped back into the van stuck an assault rifle out the window. He pointed it at the car and opened fire.

Thrower got down just in time as several shots ripped into and through the windshield. Several more bullets went into the front hood. In no time at all, the car was riddled with bullets. Thrower stayed down for a few moments until the gunfire died down. He finally picked his head up, peeking through the newly opened windshield where the glass used to be. He saw the van spin its wheels as it quickly sped out of the area.

Thrower sat up again, looking around, just to make sure there wasn't another surprise waiting for them. He didn't notice anything unusual. He then tapped Ortiz on the back.

"I think it's safe now."

Ortiz slowly sat back up. His eyes were wide open, looking as scared as scared could be. "Are they gone?"

Thrower put his gun back in its holster. "Yes, they're gone."

"Are you sure?"

"They're gone. Let's get out and survey the damage. My door's not opening so we gotta get out on your side."

"I have to get out first?"

"It'll be fine," Thrower replied. "The danger's over." He then looked into the back seat, where Angelina was still huddled over the kids on the floor. He tapped her on the shoulder. "You can get up now. It's safe."

"What did you get us into, Manuel?!"

Ortiz put his hands on his chest. "Me?! It's not my fault!"

"Well, whose fault is it, then?"

"Nobody's. It's no one's fault."

Ortiz opened his door and got out, with Thrower following him out there. Thrower took a step back and looked over the car. He put his hands on his hips, shook his head, and sighed. There was no saving this thing. Well, it could still be fixed. But it wasn't going anywhere today. Thrower even went around to the hood. The smoke rising out of it, along with the multiple bullet holes, were a clear indication this car was not going to start.

Thrower popped the hood and took a look inside to survey the damage. Heavier smoke came out as soon as the hood opened. It didn't take a genius to figure out this car wasn't going anywhere. He slammed the hood back down.

"What's the damage?" Ortiz asked.

"The damage is that it needs to be fixed."

"Can we drive it?"

Thrower shook his head. "Not today."

Ortiz put his hands on top of his head. "I can't

believe it. I can't believe it. Look what they did to my car!"

"Lucky it's just your car and not you." Angelina opened the back door to get out, but Thrower waved her back in. "Get back inside."

"Why?" she asked.

"Because standing out here there's no protection. At least in there you've got some."

Angelina agreed and got back in.

"What do we do now?" Ortiz asked.

"Well, I don't think walking is a good idea," Thrower replied. "Out in the open, too many things can go wrong."

"So what do you suggest?"

"Call someone to pick us up. Eva, Espinoza, someone."

Ortiz sighed, then took out his phone. "I will call Carlos."

"Tell him not to take his time, either," Thrower said. "We're sitting ducks out here, so I can't guarantee these guys won't make a return trip."

After Ortiz made his call, they stood by the side of the vehicle, leaning up against it.

"Carlos should be here in twenty minutes."

Thrower was keeping his head on a swivel. Though he wasn't crazy about standing out in the open like that, he didn't want to get back in the car just yet, especially when the doors on the other side weren't opening. Being cooped up in a broken-down vehicle wouldn't be too comfortable either. At least this way he could see better.

"What was this all about?" Ortiz asked.

"What do you mean?"

Ortiz pointed at the car. "This. Why did they do this?"

Thrower shrugged. "I dunno. Probably a last-ditch effort for today. They took their last shot."

"What exactly is their plan? Are they trying to kill me? Kidnap me? My family? What? Because I'm not sensing a pattern. It seems like they are all over the place. One minute they are shooting, the next minute they're not, I don't understand what they're trying to do."

Thrower couldn't deny the unusual patterns. "I don't think they're trying to kill you. Not yet, at least."

"Then why are they shooting?"

"I think it's to scare you."

Ortiz chuckled. "Well, they are doing a very good job at that, my friend."

"Look at it this way. When we first picked them up after leaving your work, they fired to scare you. To make an impact."

"Why do you not think it was to kill me?"

"Because when they got out of the van, they were coming to rough you up or take you. One or the other. They didn't get out with guns in their hands. I didn't have to disarm them. I didn't have to knock a weapon out of their hands. Nothing."

Ortiz made a face, indicating his agreement. "I buy that. But then with my family, and now this? What is the purpose?"

"I think they really were trying to take your family. Probably to hold them for ransom. But they could've killed them too if that's what they were going for. They got there before we did. They had a chance to do that if that's what they wanted. But they didn't. They were trying to drag your wife out of the house and to the van."

"Ex-wife."

Thrower rolled his eyes. "Yes, ex-wife."

"And now here?"

"I've got to assume they were here for the same purpose. To take your family and hold them hostage."

"But they tried that already and failed."

"This was a different approach," Thrower said. "Maybe they were hoping we'd crash, not be coherent, something like that. Then they could snatch the others."

"And the gunfire?"

"Well, I guess I technically started it."

Ortiz looked back at the car. "And they sure finished it."

"But also, if we look at the other two times we've come across them, I never showed them a gun. They didn't know I had one."

"So? How's that significant?"

"They might have looked at the other times, and

without seeing one, thought they could push us off the road, then take their chances again. They could have assumed I didn't have one, and thought they could take us on at gunpoint."

"So what do I do? Should I assume I am not a target physically? That they are only after my family? They're the ones who need the protection?"

Thrower shook his head. He'd learned by now to never assume anything. "I don't think it's safe to think that."

"Why not?"

"Don't forget, they did come after you first."

"Ah, yes, good point. But what good would coming after me first do, anyway?"

"They might have just been looking to show you that they were serious. To not take their demands lightly."

"And when they failed, they immediately turned towards my family to take them."

Thrower nodded. "That'd be my guess. I can't say any of that with absolute certainty, though. But it sure makes sense to me."

Ortiz sighed. "Who are these people? What do they want?"

"They're Liberation, and they want you."

"I know that much. I just wish I knew who they were and what I've done to them. Why did they choose to harass me?"

"Most extortion attempts are for two reasons," Thrower said.

"And they are?"

"They either know you personally and you pissed them off somehow. Or you're well known, and they know you have a lot of money."

"Well, I can't think of anything with the first option. The second..." Ortiz threw his hands up, not knowing what else to say.

"Didn't you say you have police friends working on it?"

"I do, but who knows if they will find anything. And who knows how long it will take. I have a feeling it will take them longer than we would."

"Can't argue that."

The two of them continued talking about the situation for the next twenty minutes, until Espinoza finally arrived. Espinoza pulled in behind the disabled vehicle and got out. He walked toward the bullet-riddled car.

"What happened?"

"It's like I told you over the phone," Ortiz said. "Let's just hurry up and get out of here before something else bad happens."

"I'll agree with that," Thrower said.

He opened the back door for Angelina and the kids to get out. They then opened the trunk to get the suitcases that they'd packed and transferred them to Espinoza's car. Once that was squared away, they got in the car and drove away from the scene.

"It's a good thing we brought Mr. Thrower in when we did," Espinoza said. "Otherwise, who knows what would have happened by now."

"Yes, very fortunate," Ortiz replied.

Thrower was in the back seat with Angelina and the kids. He heard what they were saying up front, and while it was nice to be appreciated, he wasn't paying it a whole lot of attention. He was trying to focus on that white van and what the men inside were thinking. He was trying to put himself in their position and think of what they'd do next. He couldn't be sure of what that was yet, but he was sure it would probably be soon.

11

They arrived safely back at Ortiz' home. Thrower and Espinoza helped Angelina in with her bags.

Ortiz began to tell her where she could put her things. "You can put your bags—"

Angelina was not having that, though. "If you dare tell me where I can put my things in my house, I will slap you."

"My house. It is not yours anymore."

"I wonder why that is?"

Once again, Thrower stepped in between them to prevent anything from getting started. "Why don't I help you get settled in your room?"

"Pick wherever you want," Ortiz said.

Angelina nodded at Thrower. "I want to be next to you."

"I'm not sure that's a good idea," Thrower said. "It

would probably be better if you were upstairs, just in case something happened during the night."

"I am not sleeping or staying upstairs on the same floor as him and that... whatever you call her, are sleeping. I will not be on the same floor. The safest place is next to you."

Thrower glanced over at Ortiz, who simply threw his arms up. He had no objection. As long as it didn't start an argument. Ortiz wouldn't have cared if she wanted to sleep outside if it meant no fighting.

Thrower and Espinoza once again helped with putting Angelina's bags in the room next to Thrower's. After that was settled, Thrower and Espinoza walked out back. They saw Eva swimming in the pool. They stopped and Thrower crossed his arms as they looked at her, several things running through his mind. He thought he detected Eva giving him an eye, as if she was interested.

"What do you think of her?" Thrower asked.

Espinoza looked at him curiously, thinking it was a strange question. "She's a beautiful woman."

"Not that."

"If you're thinking what I think you're thinking, man to man, I would ask you to not do it. Things could get very messy."

Now it was Thrower's turn to give him a crazy look. "What? No! No, I don't mean that. That's not even on the table."

Espinoza wiped his forehead. "Whew. Good. I'm

glad to hear you say that. Because that could make things very tricky."

"No, what I mean is, what do you think of her?"

"If you're asking personality-wise, I suppose she's fine."

Thrower kept his arms folded as he stared at her swimming. Then it dawned on Espinoza what he was asking.

He put his hand on Thrower's arm. "Wait a minute. You're not suggesting what I think you are, are you?"

"Maybe."

"Are you thinking that she might somehow be involved in these threats?"

"It crossed my mind," Thrower said.

"Oh, no, no. Couldn't be."

"Why not?"

"Because it's Eva. It's Manuel's wife."

"You may not believe this, but married couples are not always happy. And they're not always together."

"Well, that's true, but they are very much in love. I don't believe she would do something like this. I don't think she's capable. What would be her motive? She's already got everything here. A big house, money, cars, everything. What more could she want?"

Thrower looked back toward the house, thinking of Angelina. "Maybe she's afraid of winding up like his ex-wife? And all the playthings are gone."

"I see what you are thinking, but you're way off base. First of all, if you're thinking Angelina is in the poor house, you're sadly mistaken. Manuel has taken very good care of her. He pays the mortgage on that new house of hers. He bought her a new car. He didn't just dump her in the river and move on, you know?"

"Why would he do all that? The way they fight, it sounds like they're barely on speaking terms."

"Listen, they are both passionate people. Angelina hates the way their marriage ended. Perhaps Manuel feels badly about it, too. More importantly, I think it's more about the kids. He loves his children. He wants them to have a roof over their heads and transportation to wherever they want to go when he's not around, which is more than he'd like. I think it's more about making sure they're taken care of than her."

"Makes sense, I guess," Thrower said.

Espinoza put his arm out toward a table. "Let's take a seat over there."

They continued talking about the situation, while Ortiz was calling the police to make a report about everything that had happened. A few minutes later, the kids came outside with their bathing suits on and joined Eva in the pool. Thrower watched them all closely to see if their relationship seemed as good as Ortiz claimed it was.

Eva smiled at them and perked up, and the kids seemed to go to her without any hesitation. They swam together and appeared to all be having a good time. Thrower looked up at the house and saw Angelina standing there by the glass door, still inside. He knew how uncomfortable it must have been for her.

"Was their marriage good?" Thrower asked. "Before the affair."

"Yes, it was pretty good, I suppose. They didn't fight like cats and dogs if that is what you're thinking. They didn't get like that until afterwards."

"Is Manuel the type who gets a new wife every five or ten years?"

Espinoza laughed. "Who knows? We shall find out soon, I guess, huh?"

Thrower continued to watch Eva with the kids. They still seemed to be having fun. "So you don't think there's any possibility of her being involved?"

Espinoza vehemently shook his head. "Absolutely not. Look at her with those children. They adore each other."

"It does seem to be the case."

"Regardless of what you might hear from Angelina, Eva is not a monster or an evil person. Affairs, divorces, love, it all happens. Oftentimes when you don't expect it. It just is what it is. When they are here, Eva looks after those children as if they are her own."

Thrower nodded. "Good to know."

"Believe me, Eva is not part of this. I would have more reason to do that than her."

Thrower then gave him a look. The thought hadn't been lost on him. Espinoza did a double take, looking between Thrower and the pool. Considering the look

Thrower had on right now, Espinoza knew what he was thinking.

He put his hand up. "No, no, no, no, no. Do not even go there, my friend. I just said I had more motive than she does. But I don't have one either. Besides, if I were involved, do you really think I would have let Manuel hire you? I wouldn't even have gone to your hotel room. I would have just come back and pretended that you turned him down."

That was a good point. Thrower wasn't seriously considering him a suspect anyway.

"And from what you two have told me, it sounds as if you were a surprise to those men. If I were involved, don't you think I would have told them about you? I would have sent more men. I would have had them prepared for you."

Thrower nodded, then turned his attention back to the pool. "What about enemies? Manuel must have some."

"Please, you don't get to own your own company, plus have it be as successful as his, without making some enemies. And believe me, Manuel has made his share. He can be a shrewd negotiator, ruthless at times, to get the best possible deal for him and his company."

"That must have made some people angry along the way."

"Of course. But if you're thinking that someone he did business with is angry at how they were treated and is now trying to get back at him, I can't believe that would be the case. It's just business."

"People don't always view business the same way," Thrower said. "Especially if they think they're getting the short end of it. Yeah, it's just business, but if it's a deal that's making Manuel millions of dollars and the other guy's getting pennies, he's not gonna feel too great about it."

"I see your point. But I just can't see something like that."

But Thrower could. In fact, if he were putting money on it, he would've bet the over that it involved one of Ortiz' past business dealings. But Ortiz' business contacts were extensive, so finding out which one it was would be no small feat.

"Has Manuel ever been mixed up with some shady people?" Thrower asked.

"What? No. No, nothing like that."

"Even at the beginning? Maybe money was tight, things weren't looking too good, anything like that?"

Espinoza shook his head. "No. I've never seen or heard anything like that. And if it was something like that, wouldn't they have done this long before now?"

Thrower shrugged. "Depends on the repayment terms. They can sometimes shift around unexpectedly."

"No, I think it's likely what you have suggested before. There's some group out there looking for a big payday. They just know Manuel's name and figure he has money, that's all. I'm sure that's what it is."

"Maybe."

"How are we going to take care of this, though? These men, I'm sure they will try again, no?"

"Oh yeah," Thrower said. "You can be sure of that."

Thrower looked over to the house again and could see Ortiz and Angelina arguing through the glass doors.

"Do you think they'll ever get tired of doing that?"

Espinoza glanced at Thrower, then over to the house once he saw what he was looking at. "Oh." He cleared his throat. "I'm sure at some point they will. We might be old and gray by the time that happens, though."

"Wonderful."

After a few minutes, both Ortiz and Angelina disappeared from view. It wasn't long after that when Ortiz came outside. He looked a little steamed, as he usually did after he'd talked to his ex. He went over to the pool and sat down, sticking his legs in as his children and Eva came over to him. It seemed to relax him.

Ortiz stayed there for about ten minutes, then got up and went over to the table to join Thrower and Espinoza.

"What did the police say?" Espinoza asked.

Ortiz rolled his eyes. "Please. What do you think they said? They took the report and said they might be

The Bodyguard

in touch. We'll get as much help from them as we thought we would. Not enough."

"Don't you have some connections?" Thrower asked.

"With the police? Please. In this country, the police are paid badly. Some of them supplement that by taking a little something under the table, you know what I mean? You never know who you're dealing with when talking to them. You might get a good one. You also might get one who's actually involved in this. You just never know."

"The other guards are out front like I asked?"

Ortiz nodded. "Just as you directed. You really think they might try to barge in here?"

"I don't know. But at this point, I don't think we should assume anything. Or take chances."

"I agree."

"In saying that, I think we should think about Angelina's suggestion of hiring more guards."

"You're taking her side?" Ortiz asked.

"I'm not taking anyone's side. I'm taking the side of protecting everyone the best I can. And like I keep telling you, there's only one of me."

"Yes, yes, I know. Too bad we can't clone you, huh?"

Thrower laughed. "I'm not so sure that'd be a great idea."

"Do you really think we need more guards?"

"After everything that's happened today, don't you?"

Ortiz leaned on the table and put his hand on his head, looking pained just thinking about it. "Where would we even go for these men? Who do we trust?"

"Where'd you get those other two?" Thrower asked.

Ortiz looked at his friend. "Carlos took care of it."

"I simply asked a few people I thought were trustworthy," Espinoza said. "People whose opinions I respect and think highly of. They gave me a few names. That's all there was to it."

"Does this man have any more names?" Thrower asked.

"He might. I don't see why not. I only asked him for a couple of names before, but I'm sure he knows others."

"How? What's he do?"

"Well, he's retired now. He was a captain in the army."

"And you trust him?"

"Absolutely," Espinoza replied. "I've known him all my life. He was a friend of my father's. He's a good man."

"I would get in contact with him again, then. Let him know we need more names."

"How many?"

"As many as he knows," Thrower said. "Because before this is all said and done, we might need as many as he can get."

12

Before going to bed, Thrower took a walk around the grounds. He wanted to make sure there were no weak spots or holes in the fencing, something that looked like it might have been staged for a later time. Anything that looked suspicious.

Espinoza had left, but Ortiz was in the backyard with his family, taking advantage of the weather to spend time in the pool. Even Angelina and Eva were out there together, though the two of them still didn't do much talking. But at least they were occupying the same space without killing each other.

Thrower was with them for a bit before taking his stroll. He went around to the front, where one of the guards was sitting in a chair by the gate. He still looked attentive, though, as he didn't have anything in his hands to distract him. The other guard was in the house, resting, as the other two guards were rotating to keep them both fresh, but still have eyes out there.

"How's it looking?" Thrower asked.

"Very quiet. Very quiet."

"That's the way I like it."

"Do you think we're in for some trouble?"

Thrower nodded. "Yeah, I think so. I'm not sure when, but these guys will be back. It's just a question of where they make their next move."

"It could be here."

"Yeah, it could be."

"The other three attacks were three different places, right?"

"That's right," Thrower replied.

"Could be they won't try the same place twice."

"Possible. Some people won't. Can't exactly count on that right now, though."

"Well, if that's true, then the next place they hit might be here."

Thrower stared at him for a moment, before turning his attention to some trees on the other side of the iron fence. "Could be."

Thrower and the guard talked for a few more minutes, mostly about what to do if certain situations occurred. The guard was a former member of the military, though it was over ten years ago since his release. But Thrower at least figured he knew combat situations and could handle them. But ten years was also a long time to get out of practice if you didn't keep up your skills. Still, it didn't really matter whether the man was still sharp or not. He was there, and he was what they had. If something did go down, Thrower just had to hope he was good enough to handle it.

"I have a feeling the next time they attack, it will be here."

"Well, hopefully it won't be for a few more days," Thrower said. "We're gonna try to get a few more guards in here. That way if they do attack, we'll have more numbers than they do, and we can finally try to squash this thing."

"Very good. More men would be fantastic. What do you think this whole thing is about, anyway?"

"I don't know. I figure it's tied to some business dealings that Ortiz has done, but that's just a guess."

"That is what I figured too."

"Well, I'm gonna head to the back to hang out with them until they go to bed," Thrower said.

The guard nodded. "If I need you, I will call."

"Good deal."

Thrower walked around the side to get to the backyard. There was another gate that separated the front and backyards. As he got there, he saw Ortiz and the kids getting out of the pool. Angelina and Eva were sitting at tables, though separate ones. Angelina was watching her kids while Eva was on her phone. The kids then ran over to Thrower, taking a liking to him over the past few hours. They hugged him, getting water on his clothes.

"Ah, you guys are wet," Thrower said, pretending to be bothered by it.

The kids were laughing, barely standing to Thrower's waist.

"Kids, kids," Angelina said, laughing to herself.

"All right, all right, get dried off now," Thrower said, shooing them away. He walked over to Angelina's table and sat down.

She leaned over and saw some water stains on his clothes. "I'm very sorry."

Thrower waved it off. "Ah, it's only water. It'll dry."

"They've warmed up to you over the last couple of hours."

"Must've been those horseback rides I gave them."

Angelina had a smile on her face, almost forgetting why they were there in the first place. "It's helped them to put aside what happened earlier."

"Wish I could help them forget permanently. I have a feeling it's not going to be that easy, though."

"Those men, you think they will try again?"

Thrower slowly nodded. "They're gonna try something. That I can guarantee. Exactly what... that's gonna be the part that's hard to figure out. They could go anywhere or try anything right about now."

"Do you think me and the children are still a target?"

"Until we get some more clarity on everything, assume everyone's a target."

"Who is doing this? Why?"

The Bodyguard

"Well, the why is easy," Thrower answered. "Seems like money's on the top of their wish list. Who? That's the hard part."

"It must have to do with more than money."

"Not necessarily. If it's someone that your husband... ex-husband maybe treated badly in a business deal, that would be the trigger, and they wanna get back at him by taking his money. But if it's not someone he knows, it's a straight money deal."

"I wish there was more that we could do."

"We're doing it," Thrower said. "We'll meet with Espinoza's contact tomorrow, see if we can get a few more guards in here, and try to fortify this place."

"Do you believe we're safe here?"

Thrower looked at her, trying to think of whether he should tell her the truth or just the truth that would be easier for her to hear. In the end, he figured the real truth was the best way to go. It was what he usually preferred, anyway. Telling people a lie, or what they wanted to hear—which oftentimes was the same thing—didn't always work out so well. If things went bad, they could harp on the fact that they weren't leveled with. But if they knew what was coming, even if it was unpleasant, they could prepare.

By the way Thrower was wiggling around in his seat and looking uncomfortable to boot, Angelina thought she already knew the answer. But it was still better to hear the words.

Thrower leaned forward, putting his elbows on the

table as he looked around. "I don't believe anyone is safe anywhere. Now, in saying that, that doesn't mean I necessarily think an attack is imminent or they're breaking into the place tonight. But I do think it'd be a mistake to assume that they won't."

"Should I sleep with one eye open tonight?"

"I'm not sure that's necessary. But I wouldn't fall into too deep of a sleep."

"Thank you. For everything you've done for us so far. Saving us, protecting us; we feel safe in your hands."

"Don't thank me just yet," Thrower said. "Thank me when it's over."

"Hopefully that won't be too long from now."

"There's no telling with these kinds of things. I've seen them wrapped up in days, and I've seen it drag on for months."

"Months. I'm not sure I can handle that."

"You seem like you're the kind of person who can pretty much handle anything that's thrown at them."

"I don't know. I just try to be strong for my children. If I panic, they will panic. I just have to stay strong for them." The two were silent for a few minutes, with Thrower tilting his head back and closing his eyes. Angelina thought he looked tired. He must have been, considering the problems he put himself into. "How do you do this?"

Thrower opened his eyes and straightened his head. "How do I do what?"

The Bodyguard

"This. Protecting people. Putting yourself into dangerous situations. Risking your life. How do you do that over and over again?"

Thrower shrugged, not really giving it much thought. "I don't know. I guess it's just something I'm good at."

"Seems like it takes a special type of person to do that."

"I don't know about that. I don't think I'm all that special. I think I just found something I'm good at."

"How did you get drawn into this line of work? Did you choose it or did it choose you?"

"I dunno. Just happened, I guess. If you're asking if there's some sob story behind me doing this type of stuff, like someone close to me was killed, or my dog died, or something like that, it's not the case. I don't have a damaged past or anything like that. It's just as simple as me finding something I'm good at."

"How did it happen?"

"Came out of the military," Thrower said. "Just started doing some security work for other companies. Eventually made a name for myself and started doing freelance jobs."

"I understand. Do you think you'll be doing this until you're old and gray?"

Thrower laughed. "No, I don't think so. I'm looking for a beach house. Somewhere a little secluded, right on the water, some distance between me and everyone. Maybe a dog, and that's pretty much it. I don't want a mortgage or anything. I want to pay in cash. As soon as I find the place, I just wanna throw a bag of money down and be done with it."

Angelina smiled, picturing it in her mind. "A good goal to aspire to. Sounds very peaceful and relaxing."

"That's the goal. Who knows if I'll make it that far."

"You will. I get the sense that you're a survivor."

"Have been up to now. Hopefully that keeps up."

"It will."

Their conversation was interrupted when Ortiz came over, though he didn't sit down to join them. He had a towel around his neck, his swimming trunks still on.

"I think I'm going to call it a night. It's been a long day."

"Can't argue there," Thrower said.

Angelina stood up. "I think that's probably a good idea. I should get the children ready for bed and tuck myself in, too. Goodnight."

"How about you?" Ortiz asked.

Thrower nodded. "Yeah, I think it's that time. A lot to do tomorrow."

"I saw you walking the grounds. Any problems?"

"Not that I could tell yet."

"Yet. Are you expecting something?"

"I'm always expecting something," Thrower replied. "That's why I'm rarely surprised when it actually happens."

"You think something's going to happen here?"

"Well, something's going to happen somewhere. Here's as good as any."

"But not tonight, right? They wouldn't try something during the night, would they?"

Thrower shrugged. "Why wouldn't they? Are they on some kind of time schedule?"

"I wish I could make this mess go away."

"Well, you could if you want. It seems like all it takes is money."

"That, my friend, is not an option."

"I thought not. In that case, they're not going away."

"I know that. I just want to be sure that I can rest easy tonight."

"You can go rest," Thrower said. "I don't know how easy, though. I've got a feeling something's going to happen soon. Nothing definite. Just a feeling."

13

Thrower woke up and sat up in a panic. He was sweating. He instantly looked around the room. He listened, though he didn't hear a sound. It was eerily quiet. He then looked at his watch. It was just after midnight.

With a bad feeling going through him, Thrower got out of bed. He put on his shoes and then left his room. He glanced at the bedroom next to his, which had Angelina and the kids in it. He went over to it and put his ear up to the door. He didn't hear anything. He then put his hand on the knob and tried to turn it. It was locked. That was what he'd told Angelina to do. That was a good sign.

Thrower then walked out the back door and stood there, taking a look around. Nothing looked out of place. It was a cool night. Cooler than it usually was there.

Not satisfied that everything was fine, and to shake the feeling that something was off, Thrower started to walk around. He went over to the back of the fence, walking alongside it, inspecting it as he went for anything that was broken or seemed different from earlier. He didn't know why he had the feeling that something was off. Maybe it was just because of the other close calls they'd had earlier. Maybe he really did expect something else to happen that night. Or maybe he was just being overly cautious. Whatever the reason, he didn't want to be surprised.

Thrower continued walking along the fence until he got to the front. He saw the same guard, sitting in the same spot as earlier. He motioned to him, though it was more of a "we see each other" type of deal. He walked over to the guard as he inspected the fence.

"How's it looking?" Thrower asked.

"Very quiet. Almost too quiet."

"I hear ya. Any strange sounds or anything?"

The man shook his head. "No, why? You hear something?"

"No. Maybe that's what's got me. The silence."

The man laughed. "I know. I'd almost prefer a party out there."

"I don't know about that."

"Hey, only a few more hours until I get relieved."

"Counting down the time?"

"You know it. I am going to be out as soon as my head hits the pillow."

Thrower grinned. "I can imagine." He then put his hand on the man's shoulder. "Stay sharp, huh?"

"Will do."

Thrower finished his tour around the perimeter of the property, finding nothing that was odd or out of place. Everything seemed just as it was earlier. He breathed a bit easier as he went back inside to his room. He checked the knob on Angelina's door one more time, just to be sure.

He went inside his room and closed the door before conking out on his bed. It would be a short sleep, though. Only an hour later, Thrower woke up again, just like he'd done before, in exactly the same manner, including the sweating. He looked at his watch again.

Thrower looked around, sticking his ear out to try to hear the faintest of sounds. But there was nothing. He should've just chalked it up to his paranoia. But something was telling him it was more than that. He couldn't shake the feeling that something was off. But what? Was it something he'd noticed while walking along the fence? Something that he'd passed off as nothing, but subconsciously thought it was strange?

He lay back down at first, but only for a few seconds. He quickly sat back up again, unable to shake the feeling. He sighed, realizing this was the kind of night it was going to be. He had them occasionally. The kind where he couldn't sleep, constantly thinking that something was wrong. It wasn't the first time he'd felt this way, and it definitely wouldn't be the last.

Sometimes he was right and there was an issue, and sometimes he was wrong. His batting average was probably less than five hundred. But he could never shake it off. And if something happened because he didn't check it out, he wouldn't be able to live with himself. No matter how tired he was, he always had to investigate. This time was no different.

Once again, Thrower got up and left his room. He checked on the door to Angelina's room. Still locked. All good signs so far. Instead of going out the back, though, he changed it up and went out the front this time. He figured changing it up and walking in the other direction might give him a new perspective. Maybe whatever was bothering him would jump out at him this time.

Thrower walked through the quiet house, not hearing anyone else up. He went outside, and his eyes immediately gravitated to the guard. There was only one problem. He wasn't there. Thrower's eyes instantly started scanning the area, trying to find the guard. He initially thought that maybe the man had to take a leak somewhere. So Thrower remained frozen in that spot, patiently waiting for the guard to return. But he never did.

Thrower knew it didn't take that long to go to the bathroom. If that's what the guard was doing, he should have been back by now. Thrower continued looking around, expecting to find something. He wasn't sure what. A person, a tree moving, a body, something. He was positive the guard wasn't a magician and didn't disappear. But he had to be somewhere.

Thrower thought about going back inside the house to check on the guard's room. Maybe he tucked himself in early. Or maybe he used the bathroom inside, or decided to get himself a snack. But Thrower didn't hear anything while he was walking through the house on the way out there. He assumed he would've heard something if the guard was in there.

As Thrower's eyes scanned the area, he knew something else was going on here. He could feel it. Someone was out there. That's what he hadn't been able to shake. And now, with the guard missing, he figured there was.

Thrower removed the gun from his holster, then ran over to the guard's chair. He crouched down as he ran, almost expecting bullets to come flying in his direction. Thankfully, he got there without incident. Thrower then started looking at the ground, hoping to find some strange footprints, or some marks, or anything else that indicated someone else had been there.

All Thrower saw was the guard's footprints, though. Nevertheless, he noticed that they went over to the gate where they stopped once he reached the concrete path. Thrower then looked up at the gate and

The Bodyguard

noticed that it was slightly ajar. Now the hairs on his neck were really standing up. Now he knew for sure that someone was definitely out there.

With his gun out in front of him, he was ready to fire at a moment's notice, Thrower started to hear some sounds. It sounded like moaning and groaning. He pushed open the gate further to go out and investigate. He looked a little to his right and saw a pair of legs sticking out from between some bushes that covered the rest of his body.

Thrower lowered his weapon, believing he had found the guard. Just as he leaned over to check on him, he felt a powerful blow to the back of his head, knocking him to the ground. He heard some voices, though they were faint, as they apparently started moving away from him.

He wasn't knocked unconscious, thankfully, but he sure did have a big headache. Knowing something was planned at the house, Thrower knew he couldn't lay there and wait to feel better. There wasn't time. The people in the house needed him.

He attempted to get up, pushing himself up on his hands and knees like he was doing push-ups. Almost instantly he felt another wallop on the back of his head. He put his hand on the back of his head, the pain almost unbearable. Whoever this group was, they must've left someone there to make sure that Thrower didn't interfere in their plans.

At least they didn't put a couple of bullets in him,

which they easily could have done. But that was a small consolation, knowing that other people were depending on him to keep them safe. And as it looked right now, he had failed.

Thrower remained still for a few moments, trying to figure out how he was going to get out of this. The guard was slightly to his right. And the blows felt like they came from his left, but not straight to his left. It felt like an angle, like it was slightly behind him.

He had to make a move quickly. There wasn't time to dilly-dally. Trying to ignore the throbbing pain that his head seemed to be engulfed in, Thrower quickly spun around, kicking at where he hoped his attacker was. He had to hope that he guessed right, because if he didn't, he was sure to get another painful response.

Luckily, Thrower was right on the mark. He kicked the man's legs, who hadn't suspected the attack. The man's legs buckled slightly, though he didn't go down. But it gave Thrower enough time to jump back to his feet. And once he was, that was all the space that Thrower needed.

Though the other man did have a gun in his hands, it didn't do him much good. Thrower immediately went on the attack, completely overwhelming the man with several punches to his face. The man was stunned and dropped his weapon. A few seconds later, Thrower dropped him, too.

Moments later, Thrower's worst fears were realized. He heard screaming coming from the house. It sounded like Angelina. He raced into the house and flipped on the lights as soon as he entered. There was no need to try to be quiet or invisible now. Being able to see what he was up against was the priority now.

As soon as he flicked on the lights, he saw Angelina running toward the back door, which was now open. She was still hysterical, screaming, and now running outside. Thrower ran after her. Just as he got to the door, he heard gunshots. He stopped and peeked outside.

Angelina was now hiding behind a chair, as the bullets were apparently meant for her. She got up again, though, and started going after whoever had broken in. They had one of her children. And she didn't care what was being done to her, she had to make sure they didn't take her daughter.

Thrower emerged from the door and ran towards Angelina's position. As soon as he did, the kidnappers opened up again, firing at both of them. Angelina had nowhere to go and would have been mowed down if Thrower hadn't been able to save her.

Thrower ran straight toward her and made a flying tackle, as if he were a middle linebacker, sending them both crashing into the pool. Luckily it was a softer landing than the concrete. Just as they flung themselves into it, several more bullets ripped into the water, though they thankfully missed either target.

As the kidnappers fired a couple more shots, Thrower pushed Angelina's head under water to try to keep her out of range. It seemed to work, as the kidnappers seemed more intent on getting away than they were on killing either of them. Right now, they just wanted to get away with their target, which was apparently the child.

Within seconds, it was all over. The kidnappers had disappeared into the night. Thrower and Angelina slithered their way out of the pool, though they stayed on the ground, both looking like they had lost a ton of energy. Every light in the house seemed to turn on, and everybody poured out of the house to check on what was happening. They saw Thrower and Angelina on the ground and rushed over to them.

"Oh my God, what happened?" Ortiz asked.

"They took her!" Angelina yelled. "They took her!"

Thrower was still down, face first, and hardly moving. They then noticed the redness on the back of his head. He was bleeding from the blows he'd taken earlier. Most likely from the butt-end of a gun. Ortiz and Eva went over to Thrower to tend to him.

"It looks like you got the worst of it, my friend," Ortiz said, helping Thrower sit up.

Thrower was able to sit up, but put his hand on the back of his head. His hand quickly became red. He wasn't thinking about his own injuries, though. He was thinking about the daughter of his client. "Not the worst of it. Not even close."

Ortiz looked over to his wife. "Go get the bandages."

As Eva went inside to get the supplies to clean Thrower's wounds, all Thrower kept thinking about was the little girl who had been taken. That's all he was upset about. He didn't care about his head. Didn't care about being hurt. Didn't care about anything other than feeling like he had failed this family.

Failure was something that did not sit well with Thrower. When he failed, he got angry. And when he got angry, other people started paying the price. This time would be no different. The people that took that little girl, they would pay the price.

14

Thrower was sitting outside at one of the tables, a bandage on the back of his head. He had his elbows on the table and his hands pressed against his forehead. A few seconds later, Ortiz came around through the side gate with the other guard. Thrower looked over at him, pleased to see that he wasn't killed, though it looked like he was sporting a bad end of it, too. The guard was also holding his head. Ortiz brought him over to the table, the guard sitting across from Thrower.

"I am sorry," Pedro said.

Thrower flicked his hand in the air as he sat back. He wasn't in any position to talk.

"I failed. There is no excuse for my actions."

"You're not the only one," Thrower said.

Pedro looked around. "What about Fernando?"

Thrower squinted, not even giving the second

guard much thought until now. It was a good question, though. Where was Fernando? Why didn't he put up any effort to stop the kidnapping? He would have been closer than either Thrower or Pedro, considering they were both out front by the gate. But Thrower hadn't seen him at all during this whole situation.

"Manuel," Thrower said. "Where is Fernando?"

Ortiz looked perplexed as well, as he threw his arms out. "I don't know. I haven't seen him."

"You don't think that's strange?"

"I don't know. I assumed you had him doing something."

Thrower shook his head. "He shouldn't be doing anything but standing guard."

Ortiz put his finger in the air as he started to back away. "Let me go check."

"How'd they get you?" Thrower asked his partner.

Pedro shook his head, still not believing what had happened. "I was sitting there in my chair. And then I started to hear noises." He waved his hand in the air to illustrate how small they were. "Nothing big. Just little noises. It sounded like someone brushing up against the leaves and bushes. Maybe an animal or something. Since nothing else was going on, I decided to go have a look. I get out there, and pow, I immediately feel something come down on the back of my head. I must have passed out because I don't remember anything that happened after that until Mr. Ortiz helped me."

Thrower nodded. "Yeah. I came out to look for you and wound up with the same fate."

"What are we going to do?"

"We gotta get that kid back, that's what."

"But how? We don't even know who these people are or where they are."

"We have to find out," Thrower said.

They sat there for a few more minutes, talking about everything that had gone wrong over the last hour. Then Ortiz came outside, his arm around Angelina's shoulder. They walked over to the table. Once they got closer, Angelina broke free of him and ran over to Thrower. She put her hands on his arms.

"We have to get Rosa back! Please, we have to get her back!"

Thrower stood up and put his arms around her. He knew she was hurting. "We'll get her back. I promise you, we'll get her back."

Angelina looked up at him, hope in her eyes. "You will try to get her?"

"I won't try. I will."

"I've checked the entire property," Ortiz said. "Fernando isn't anywhere to be found."

"That's not good," Pedro said.

Thrower glanced at him. "No, it's not good."

"What does that mean? Ortiz asked. "Where is he?"

"It means he either heard all the commotion and took off, or..."

"Or he's working with them," Pedro said.

The Bodyguard

Thrower nodded. "Or he's working with them."

Ortiz angrily slapped himself in the arm. "I am the one who brought him in here." He hit himself in the shoulder again, appearing to be chewing himself out. "I can't believe I would allow this to happen."

"Well, don't go beating yourself up just yet. We don't know for sure he was helping them. It's still possible he heard everything that was going on and just decided he didn't want to get involved. Maybe he figured this wasn't for him."

Ortiz rubbed his hands all over his face, appearing exasperated. "I don't know where to turn to or who to trust anymore. My driver, my guard, who's next?"

Thrower looked at Pedro. "Well, it looks like you know you got two people here you can trust."

Ortiz bobbed his head. "Yes, yes, I thank you both for that. I know you are both loyal and willing to risk your life, and for that, I am very thankful. But that still doesn't change the fact that I feel like the walls are closing in. And now my daughter has been taken. I feel like I'm being squeezed." He balled his fists and motioned to emphasize the point, though it wasn't really necessary.

Eva came out of the house and eventually came over to her husband, standing beside him. "Aren't you still meeting with Carlos tomorrow?"

"Yes, but even if he gives me more guards, that only solves part of the problem. It still doesn't get Rosa back."

"I'm not meeting with anyone," Thrower said.

"But you thought it was a good idea," Ortiz replied.

"That was before this. Isn't this guy that Carlos knows the same guy who supplied you with Fernando?"

"Yes."

"It might be no fault of his own, and maybe Fernando's not even mixed up with them, but I don't know if we can really take the chance of bringing in five more guys if there's any kind of doubt hanging over their heads."

Ortiz put his hand over his chin as he thought about it. "You're right. It's a chance we cannot take. But what else do we do? Now we're down another man. How do we fight these people?"

"Leave that to me. I'll figure it out."

"But how?" Ortiz asked.

"We have to do some digging on this," Thrower replied. "I would imagine you'll get a ransom demand relatively soon."

"And I would pay it. If it gets my daughter back and ends all this nonsense, I would gladly pay it. I am done with this. I just want to get back to a normal life. I want me and my family to feel safe again. This is no kind of life for them."

"I agree with that. But even if you pay, like you've said before, it makes you an easier target from now on. Now they know you'll buckle."

The Bodyguard

"What else can I do? I cannot leave my child in the hands of a stranger."

"I'll fix it."

"How? What can you do? You said before you only do protection. That you do not try to figure out who's behind all of this. That's not your area of concern."

Thrower felt the back of his head, feeling a twinge of pain. "I may have undersold myself a little. I don't always just sit back and wait. Sometimes I say that to help keep expectations lower. Sometimes you have to fight fire with fire. And sometimes... the best defense is a good offense."

"That all sounds well and good," Ortiz said. "But how can you fight against something that is invisible? We don't know a thing about these people. And now we're down another man on top of it."

"You're a wealthy man, right?"

"Yes."

"You must have some powerful friends that go along with that."

"Not powerful enough to get me out of this mess," Ortiz replied.

"You have friends with the police," Eva said.

Ortiz put his arm up, like he was blowing off the suggestion. "Ah, the police. Police in this country, you never know who to trust or turn to."

"What about the government?" Thrower asked. "Do you know anyone there who could help?"

"I have some passing acquaintances."

"It's better than none."

"I mean, I guess I could see what I could do. But I wouldn't get your hopes up."

"What about using the police to our advantage?" Thrower asked.

"I already told you, the police here, you never know who to trust. And there are so many layers to police corruption here, it goes far beyond what foreigners understand."

"Well, if they're corrupt, couldn't you use that money to help persuade them to work for you?"

Ortiz stared at him for a moment. It was something he hadn't considered. "That is a slippery slope, my friend. Once you start in that type of world, can you get out?"

Thrower knew what he was saying. Once people knew he was willing to pay for bribes, would they come around again? Or would they make him the victim at some other point down the road?

But Thrower knew Ortiz was right. The police corruption in Mexico went far beyond his understanding. Even though Thrower had been to the country many times and had heard often about the police corruption problem, he didn't often have to deal with it. He knew that bribes and payoffs were a normal occurrence in some police circles. But in this case, with a little girl's life on the line, he figured all bets were off. Everything should be on the table for consideration now.

"I can start asking around, seeing if there is anyone who can help for a fee," Ortiz said. "I just don't know if it will do any good."

Thrower nodded. "All you can do is try to see where it leads."

"And if it leads nowhere?"

"Then we'll have to try something else."

"What else is there?"

Thrower looked over at Angelina, who was now sitting at the table, her head down and buried into her arms as she stretched across it.

"Then maybe it'll be time we get a little high tech."

"What does that mean?" Ortiz asked.

"There's cameras around, right? Maybe one of them will have picked up the van? Maybe we can see where it's gone. Or even a shot at some of their faces."

"Do you have experience in that sort of thing? Doesn't that require some type of, uh, computer knowledge to acquire that type of thing?"

"I don't, no," Thrower said. "But I may know someone who does."

15

They'd been waiting through the night and into the morning. They were sure a ransom call was coming at some point. It had to be. They wouldn't have taken Rosa otherwise. If they were planning to kill her, they would have done it already. Unless they were going for something dramatic. Thrower didn't even want to entertain that possibility. But there were some groups who would kidnap someone, then dismember them and send them back in pieces as a message. They had to hope this group wasn't that violent.

They'd all been sitting around, just waiting for that call. Angelina seemed the most restless, as expected.

"Are you sure we shouldn't call the police?" she asked.

Ortiz looked at Thrower.

Thrower shrugged. "Calling the police is up to you. But I can tell you that the kidnappers are going to tell you not to talk to them or bring them in. And if they're as untrustworthy as you believe they are, I'm not sure there's a difference."

Angelina looked back to her ex-husband. He seemed to be considering it.

"No. No, we will handle this ourselves. We have Nate. That is enough. I don't trust the police to bring them in and have them rescue our daughter. We can do it."

"This is Rosa's life we're talking about," Angelina replied. "Everything should be on the table and considered."

"I agree."

"That means the police."

"And what if we go to them and they do nothing? Or what if we go to the wrong one and they extort more money? You know as well as I do the corruption that goes on here. You're just as easily liable to walk into more trouble as you are not."

"But this is our daughter's life."

"I know. Don't you think I'm well aware of that?" Ortiz paced around for a minute, before thinking of something that his bodyguard had mentioned before. "You said something earlier about knowing someone who may be able to help with this."

Thrower nodded. "I did. I sent him a message."

"And have you heard back from him?"

"He said he was in the middle of something. He'll call me back when he's able."

Ortiz put his arm up. "When will that be? We're not exactly swimming with time here."

"Time's all we got right now."

"Who is this man? Reliable? Some kind of expert?"

"Yes in both cases," Thrower answered.

"What does he do?"

Thrower made a face, like he was struggling with an answer. He was, really. "He's... very experienced in this type of thing."

"Is he in law enforcement or government or something?"

"Uh, yeah, you could say something close to that."

It wasn't too far from the truth. David Jones used to be an ex-NSA agent, so he was well-versed in finding information that was supposed to be hidden. And in his current job as the Silencer's trusted partner, he was very experienced with these types of situations. But Thrower didn't even know if he was available at the moment. Jones was often busy, following up with thousands of pieces of information that flowed through his computer every day.

Still, if Jones wasn't available, Thrower did know of one other hacker that he had worked with before. But he was willing to wait a few more hours to see if Jones was available soon.

"Have you worked with this man before?" Ortiz asked.

"Yeah. He's really good. The best I've ever encountered."

The Bodyguard

"And you think he can help us?"

"I think if anyone can find that van... it's him."

"I pray to God he'll be able to do it soon."

The room filled with silence over the next few minutes as everyone sat down, thinking, praying, or a combination of both. It was broken by the sound of Ortiz' phone ringing. He eagerly answered.

"Yes?"

"Manuel Ortiz," a male voice said.

"Yes, I am here."

"Would you like to get your daughter back in one piece?"

"Yes, of course. Whatever you want. I just want her back."

"Two million pesos. That's what it will take to get her back."

Ortiz hesitated at hearing the high price and cleared his throat. He wasn't going to balk or try to negotiate, though. He knew better. "OK. Fine. When and where?"

"We'll give you the details later. Have the money ready by five o'clock."

Ortiz glanced over at Thrower. "Five o'clock?"

Thrower made a few hand motions at him, wanting him to keep the man talking longer. He actually hoped that Ortiz would be able to delay the drop for another day. Doing the exchange later that day didn't give them much time.

"I'm not sure I can get the money in time," Ortiz said.

"You better."

"It's a lot of money in a short amount of time."

"That's your problem."

"Please, I'm willing to do what you ask. I just want to make sure I can get all the money."

"Do it."

"Even five or six hours after that would be helpful," Ortiz said.

"Five o'clock. Have it ready. If it's not, you won't see your daughter again. Alive, that is."

"OK. Five o'clock. I'll make sure I have it."

"I hope so. For her sake. Oh yeah, and when we do the exchange, you make sure you leave the big guy behind."

"What big guy?" Ortiz asked.

"Don't get cute. You know who we're talking about. If we even see that guy when we make the exchange, even if he's three blocks away, we'll cut your daughter's throat. And then we'll come over and do the same to the rest of your family. The same goes for the police. If we see the police, or the big guy, you'll be attending a mass funeral."

The man hung up, not waiting for a response, though Ortiz kept the phone pressed to his ear for a little while longer. He finally was able to pull the phone away, letting his arm hang down. He looked to be in shock.

The Bodyguard

"What did he say?" Angelina asked.

"Two million pesos. By five o'clock today."

"Where?" Thrower asked.

Ortiz shook his head. "He didn't say. He said he would call later."

"What else did he say?"

"Not much. He just said that when we do the exchange, that you must stay behind."

"Me?"

Ortiz nodded. "He said if they see you or the police..." He glanced over at Angelina. "If they see either, they'll cut Rosa's throat."

Angelina put her hand over her mouth. "Oh my God."

"Why? Why do they not want you there?"

"Seems fairly obvious," Thrower replied. "They view me as a threat. They think if I'm there that something might go wrong for them."

"What do we do?" Angelina asked.

"Can you get the money?" Thrower said.

"Yes, that's not really a problem," Ortiz answered. "You think we should go through with it?"

Thrower took a deep breath before answering. That was a loaded question without a good answer. Two million pesos was the equivalent of about a hundred thousand dollars. The money wasn't really the issue, though. Ortiz had that and much more. The real question was whether the kidnappers were actually going to go through with the exchange at all. And whether Rosa was even still alive.

"Look, your daughter's life could be on the line here," Thrower said. "All I can do is advise you of your options. What you do after that is up to you."

"Whatever you think is best," Ortiz said.

"You can do exactly what he says. Go where they want you to go, drop off the money, and hope they live up to their word and give Rosa back to you."

"Hope? You think they are lying?"

"At the end of the day, there are never any guarantees with these things. You can do the deal and hope it's on the up-and-up. You also have to be aware that they could be luring you into a trap and wind up taking you, too. Or they might draw you in, take the money, then kill you."

Ortiz gulped, not liking what he was hearing.

Thrower continued. "There's also the possibility that they have no intention of giving Rosa back for a variety of reasons."

"They won't give her back?" Angelina asked.

"I just said it's a possibility. They might do as they say. They might take the money and keep her and ask for another payment later. Or there's the other possibility. The one I don't even want to think about."

"What possibility?" Ortiz asked.

Thrower hesitated to even say it. But he knew he had to prepare them for the worst, even if it wasn't likely. He couldn't be sure on this, though. "The possibility that she's already dead. Or they'll kill her once they get the money."

"Oh, no," Angelina said, worrying even more, if that was possible.

"I'm not saying it's likely. I just want you to know everything that might happen. Whether it's a ninety percent chance or a one percent chance. You need to know what could happen."

"I understand."

"Now, we can mitigate those risks if I'm there," Thrower said.

"But they said not to," Ortiz said.

"Whether you choose to include me in this or not, I'll leave it up to you. If I'm there, you'll have a certain level of protection. If something goes down unexpectedly, I might be able to do something."

"But what if they do see you?" Angelina asked. "Would they really kill our baby?"

Thrower could only shake his head. "I don't know. All I can do is tell you there are risks in either case. They could kill her or Manuel whether I'm there or not. At least if I'm there, there's a fighting chance. If I'm not... they can pretty much do whatever they want. You will be at their mercy."

Ortiz gulped. He knew there were risks with whatever route they decided to take. All they could do now was try to figure out which was the most acceptable. And which one would lead to the safe return of their daughter.

"What do you think is best?"

Thrower would almost always go with the option that included his presence. This time was no different. "I think I should be there."

Angelina had already made up her mind on which direction they should take. "But they said—"

"I know they said I shouldn't be there," Thrower said. "I can blend in. I know how to stay in the background. I don't have to be front and center. Me being there is the best way to keep Rosa and Manuel safe."

"Manuel, we cannot do anything that might jeopardize Rosa's life," Angelina said. "Whatever these people say, we must do it. We cannot deviate and risk her life. No matter what."

"What about Pedro?" Eva finally asked. "If they said no police and no to Nate, did they not mention Pedro? Did they say you could not bring anyone for protection?"

Ortiz put his hand on his chin, thinking about his conversation with the kidnapper. "You are right. They didn't say to come alone. They just said no police and don't bring the big guy. Perhaps this is a way to bridge the difference."

Thrower shrugged, though he didn't feel comfortable with their solution. He wasn't going to argue their call, though. It wasn't that he thought Pedro wasn't capable of handling things if the situation went sideways, but he didn't know that he could, either. It was more of how confident he was in his own abilities.

The Bodyguard

He'd been through these things before. He was sure Pedro hadn't.

After thinking about it more, Ortiz settled on his decision. "Yes, that's what we'll do. Unless they say explicitly to come alone, I will bring Pedro. I cannot risk Rosa's life by being defiant. I hope you understand."

Thrower nodded. "I do. I just hope it goes the way you want it to."

He knew that was far from a given, though. In fact, in his experience, things rarely went as expected. Especially in situations like this. He just had to hope that if something went down, Ortiz and Pedro would be able to handle it without him.

16

Thrower accompanied Ortiz to the bank, even though it probably wasn't necessary. It was unlikely anything was going to happen to him now. Not when the kidnappers were close to getting the money they wanted. Still, it was always possible Ortiz could've been targeted by another group who just happened to have their eyes on the bank he was taking money out of.

Pedro stayed back at the house with the rest of the family, just in case someone made a move on them, though Thrower figured there was a pretty remote chance at this point. As they left the bank, Thrower's phone rang. It was the call he'd been waiting for.

"Hey, thanks for getting back to me."

"No problem," Jones said. "I'm sorry it took me so long. We were in the middle of a rather difficult situation. It took a little longer than I thought."

The Bodyguard

"It's fine. I just appreciate you taking some time for me."

"Anything for you, Nate. You know you're basically one of us now."

"Thanks. I do appreciate that."

"So what's the situation? I assume you're not calling just to shoot the breeze?"

"I wish I were," Thrower said, getting into the passenger seat of one of Ortiz' other vehicles. "I've got a problem down here in Mexico."

"Be glad to help if I can."

"I've been hired to protect a businessman down here who's been getting threats. Last night, they broke into the house and took his daughter."

"Oh no."

"We've got no leads on who this group is," Thrower said. "I was wondering and hoping that you would be able to work some of your magic and pick up this van on a camera or something? Something that would indicate who they are, or where they are."

"A van?"

"A white van." Thrower could hear Jones typing in the background.

"Tell me everything you know. The more I can input here, the better off we'll be."

"All I know is a white van. There have been no plates on it. Just a plain white van."

"That is actually not as bad as it seems," Jones replied. "Instead of struggling to catch a glimpse of a van's plate, now all we have to do is find one that doesn't have any. That actually helps it to stand out and identify. What time did this happen?"

"Must've been around one, I think. Definitely between midnight and two." Thrower also gave him Ortiz' address. He could still hear Jones feverishly typing away.

"OK. That should be enough to start with."

"You think you'll be able to pick them out with just that?"

"Well, it really all depends on two things," Jones answered. "The direction the van took, and whether there's any cameras on that route."

He could hear in Thrower's voice that things didn't seem to be going his way. Of course, a child missing tended to depress anybody. It always did when he was looking for one, too.

"How much time do you think you have on this?"

Thrower sighed. "Tough to say. They're asking for a ransom demand, which is scheduled to go down later today."

"You hope to get this information before then?"

"I don't know. I'm just... nervous about this whole thing. They specifically requested for me not to be there."

"That doesn't sound good."

"No, it doesn't."

"Do you need assistance on this?" Jones asked. "I might be able to send Michael or Chris down."

"I don't want to take you guys away from what you're doing."

"Like I said, we just wrapped something up, so for the moment, we're in the clear. I could always ask one to go down and keep the other here just so we're covered. You've helped us in the past, so we'd be delighted to return the favor."

"They wouldn't get here in time," Thrower said.

The prospect of either Mike Recker or Chris Haley coming down to help certainly excited him. He knew he could trust them both, much more than he would anyone else who showed up. Not only could he trust them, but he knew their talent and skills. There would be no worrying if one of them were to appear. But as he said, there was no time. Even if Recker or Haley left at this exact minute, it was a six- or seven-hour flight at best. Neither would get there before the drop was scheduled to go down.

"Well, if things go sideways..."

"Let me keep it on the back burner," Thrower said. "Like you say, if things go down sideways at this exchange, maybe I could use some backup."

"Do you have anyone else you can trust down there? Anyone else on your team?"

Thrower chuckled. "Right now I'm a team of two. My client already hired a couple of bodyguards before I got here, and one of them just split. So we're pretty light right now."

"Understood. Sounds like you could use a hand."

"As long as it's not a burden on you, and if it's necessary."

"Well, as you say, if things don't turn out the way you want, let us know."

"Thanks," Thrower said. "Maybe if you can get me the location of that van, I can spoil the party ahead of time, and then I won't need any additional help."

"I'll do my best. But as you know, there are no guarantees. Nonetheless, I'll let you know the moment I learn something. And if I don't, I'll let you know that, too."

"Appreciate the help, David."

As soon as Thrower hung up, Ortiz started peppering him with questions. He was doing his best to listen to the conversation.

"What did he say?"

"He's gonna start looking for the van," Thrower replied.

"How long will that take?"

"All depends. It's gonna take some time to find some cameras, then hack his way into them, then hope that the van passed through some of them. It takes a while to put it all together."

"Do you think it could be done before the meeting?"

Thrower shrugged. "Possible. We can't count on that, though."

As they started discussing their possible options again, Ortiz' phone rang. It was an unfamiliar number.

The Bodyguard

He looked at it for a moment, unsure about whether he should answer it. Eventually, he decided he should, and pulled over to the side of the road. He put it on speaker.

"Yes?"

"Looks like the meeting time has been pushed up," the male voice said. It was the same voice that Ortiz had spoken to earlier.

"Pushed up? What do you mean? You said five o'clock."

"Things change. Now it's sooner."

"How much sooner?"

"Now."

"What?" Ortiz looked over at Thrower, worried about this latest development. "Now? It's too soon."

"Why? You've already got the money."

Ortiz' eyes widened. They were watching him. That's the only way they could have known he had the money already. He instantly looked in the rearview mirror, but he didn't see anything out of the ordinary. Thrower looked around as well. He didn't see anything, either.

"I just... I wasn't ready yet," Ortiz said. "I was preparing myself for later."

"Well, you can prepare yourself for now."

Thrower tapped Ortiz on the arm. As Ortiz looked over at him, Thrower started mouthing the words to him. He wanted Ortiz to ask for proof of life. He wanted him to speak to Rosa before doing anything.

Thrower wanted to be sure that she was still alive. If she wasn't, there was no point in continuing the situation any further. That was the key to everything from this moment forward.

"I want to speak to Rosa," Ortiz said.

"She's fine."

Ortiz glanced at Thrower, who motioned for him to keep asking. "I need to speak to Rosa. I need to know she's OK first."

There was silence on the other end of the phone. Ortiz wasn't sure what was happening. The line hadn't gone dead. Then, he heard Rosa's voice. All she said was hello. Then the kidnappers took the phone away from her again.

"Rosa!" Ortiz said, wanting to hear her voice again.

The man came back on the line. "There. She's alive. So we do the deal now, or we don't do it at all."

"Fine. OK. Whatever you want. Where do you want me to go?"

"Home."

"What?" Ortiz said. "I thought you wanted to do it now."

"We do. But remember what we said? No big guy. We know he's with you right now."

Thrower looked around again. There was no doubt in either of their minds that they were either being watched and followed now, or they were from Ortiz' house on the way to the bank. Maybe they stopped following after they saw Thrower and Ortiz leave the bank. In any case, the kidnappers knew.

"OK," Ortiz said. "I'll go home. Then what?"

"Then we'll call you with further instructions. But you leave the big guy at home. If we see him, the girl's dead. Remember that. Once you arrive at the meeting place, we'll inspect the car. If we see the big guy in the back seat, or in the trunk, or even following in another car, you won't see your daughter alive again."

"I'll remember."

"Good. We'll talk soon."

Ortiz hung up and sighed. Thrower continued to look around, though he still saw no sign of them being actively followed. They could have been watching from a distance, he thought. It didn't really matter now. The situation was what it was. They had to deal with it.

"I guess that seals it," Ortiz said. "There can be no deviations. They are watching our every move."

"Yeah, seems like it. From here on out, be prepared for anything."

"Where do you think they will make me go?"

"Not sure," Thrower replied. "Wherever it is, I'm sure it'll be a remote spot. Not a lot of people to watch. And somewhere they can see everything."

"I just want Rosa back. I'll do whatever is necessary."

"I get it. You just need to be careful out there. You need to watch your six. One thing's for sure, they obviously are."

17

They arrived back at Ortiz' place and waited for the next phone call. Angelina was waiting in the corner, sitting on a chair, her hands clasped together in front of her face. She looked like she was praying. Eva was also sitting in a chair, though in the opposite direction of Angelina. Ortiz was pacing the room. Thrower and Pedro were standing next to each other, against a wall, facing everyone. Then Ortiz' phone rang again. He eagerly answered.

"Yes? I'm here."

"Leave now," the voice said.

"Where? Where am I going?"

"Just get in your car and drive. We'll call you again once you're on the road. And don't forget the conditions regarding the big guy."

"You don't have to worry about him," Ortiz said. "I give you my word he will stay here. I will not jeopardize my daughter's safety. She is the only thing that matters. As long as you keep your end of the deal, I will keep mine."

"Good. Start driving."

Ortiz hung up, then looked at Pedro. "We must go."

"Where to?" Angelina asked.

"They did not say yet. They will call me again once I am on the road."

Thrower nodded. He knew exactly what the kidnappers were doing. They were going to be watching Ortiz' car, making sure nobody was following him. Once they were sure that Ortiz was alone, and after they probably made him stop a few times, then they'd give him the final destination. But only once they were positive there would be no surprises in store. Surprises like Thrower suddenly appearing. The kidnappers were playing it smart, much to Thrower's chagrin. They obviously didn't want to tangle with him again.

Pedro was ready and quickly went out to the car to get it started. He also brought his rifle with him, which he put down on the front seat. Thrower, along with the others, accompanied Ortiz outside to the car.

"Best chance you have is just doing what they say," Thrower said. "Don't agitate them. Just give them the money, grab Rosa, and get back here as quick as you can."

Ortiz nodded and shook his hand. "Will do." He then kissed Eva. "I'll be back soon."

"Please bring her back," Angelina said.

Ortiz put his hand on hers. "I will. Safe and sound."

Thrower went over to Pedro, who was already behind the wheel. "Stay alert out there." He leaned through the window to talk privately with him, making sure the others couldn't hear him. "There's no guarantee they're gonna give the girl back. And the whole thing might be a setup. So you need to stay sharp at all times."

"Eyes like an eagle," Pedro replied.

Ortiz got in the car, and they slowly drove away from the property. Once they were out of sight, the others went back inside. Everyone seemed to gravitate outside, with Angelina's son going in the pool. Eva joined him in there, as Thrower and Angelina went over to one of the tables and sat down.

"What do you think will happen?" Angelina asked.

"Hopefully, the exchange will go down without a problem and they'll be back with Rosa in an hour or two."

"You don't sound convinced."

Thrower didn't want to get her hopes up. But he wasn't trying to destroy them either. He honestly didn't know how this was going to go down. It might go off without a hitch. And it might wind up being a disaster. There was just no way to tell yet.

"Look, there's always a chance of these things going sideways," Thrower said. "That's just the nature of it. But there's also plenty of times when things go down exactly the way they're supposed to. We just have to hope this is one of those times."

"What is your feeling?"

Thrower cleared his throat, not wanting to tell her his true feelings. It wouldn't have done her any good to hear them. "I think it'll be fine."

Angelina could tell that he had no conviction in his voice. But she wasn't going to press him on it any further. She just had to hope right along with him that everything would turn out fine in the end. That's all they could do. Was hope.

Ortiz had been in the car for over thirty minutes. The kidnappers had called three different times, each time telling him to drive to a different location. And each time he got there, they told him to drive somewhere else.

Ortiz wasn't sure if they were just playing games with him, or they were just trying to make sure that nobody was following him. In either case, he was starting to get frustrated. He just wanted to get this over with and bring his daughter back home.

They had pulled over to the side of the road, waiting for the phone to ring again. Ortiz looked around, though they were in a spot without much traffic. Maybe this was it, he thought. Not many people or cars to get in the way. Then his phone rang.

"You're doing good."

"When is this going to end?" Ortiz asked. "I've done as you asked, I've followed every instruction, I just want to get this over with and get my daughter. Enough with the games."

"It's enough when we say it's enough."

With Ortiz distracted on the phone, and Pedro too, they never saw or heard anyone approaching the car. They both spun around as they heard the back door open. They saw another man sliding onto the back seat. He had a gun in his hand.

"The man who's now in your car will tell you where to go from here. Listen to his directions carefully and don't deviate. If you don't make it here in the time it should take, or something happens to him, we won't try again."

"I understand," Ortiz said. He hung up, then looked at the man that was now behind them. "Where to?"

"Just drive," the man answered.

Pedro pulled onto the road again, the stranger telling him where to turn just before they got to the street they needed to be on. They drove for another thirty minutes before finally getting to where the kidnappers apparently were. It was just off a main road, and there was a building there, though it looked like it hadn't been kept up for a while. And there was nothing but dirt for as far as they could see, except for the paved road.

"Looks like we're here," the man in the backseat said. "Time to get out."

Ortiz and Pedro slowly got out of the car. They each took a look around. It wasn't exactly a comfortable situation for either of them. They were in the middle of nowhere.

"Where is Rosa?" Ortiz asked.

"Just relax. They'll be coming."

A minute or two later, another car drove over to them. It was that same white van that they knew oh so well by now. The driver and a man in the passenger side got out, walking over to Ortiz.

"You got the money?" the man from the passenger side asked. He was also the leader of the group.

"Where is Rosa?" Ortiz replied.

The man glanced back and pointed with his thumb back at the van. "She's in there."

"I want to see her."

"Not without the money. Where is it?"

Ortiz stared at him for a moment, but then reached inside the front seat and pulled out a briefcase. He handed it over to the kidnapper.

"It's all there."

The man put it on the hood and opened it. A smile crept over his face, seemingly pleased.

"Now, where is Rosa?" Ortiz asked.

"Well, we kind of neglected to bring her."

"What?! That was not the deal."

"We decided to change it."

In a fit of rage, Ortiz tried to strike the man, but the man punched Ortiz in the stomach. He then nailed Ortiz in the back, up near the shoulders, causing Ortiz to fall onto his knees.

Pedro started to intervene, but he was quickly taken care of too. The man from the backseat struck him in the back of the head, putting Pedro on his knees as well.

The leader of the group squatted down, just in front of Ortiz as he tried to catch his breath. It was almost like he was taunting him.

"You see, we don't like to be ignored."

"What?" Ortiz said, getting back up to his feet. "I've done what you asked."

"No, you haven't. We sent you three messages. And you ignored all of them. And then you went and got some big bodyguard, thinking that he would save you. He would protect you. Well, you thought wrong. Guess what? Nobody can protect you from us."

"I've brought you the money. What else do you want? I just want Rosa back."

"Now, if you want your daughter back, it's going to cost you extra."

"What?"

"Now the price has doubled. Bring another suitcase. Just like this one. Tomorrow. We'll be in touch."

"Wait, no," Ortiz said, grabbing the man by the shirt.

The man quickly shook Ortiz off him, then delivered a couple of punches that sent Ortiz sprawling to the ground.

"Why?" Ortiz asked, feeling his face for signs of blood, of which there was thankfully none. "Why are you doing this?"

The man stared at Ortiz. "You don't remember me, do you?"

Ortiz shook his head. "No. Who are you?"

The man laughed. "That's what I figured. You've never really looked at anyone and noticed them. Not unless it made you money. And even the people who have made you money, you still didn't notice them. Looks like that hasn't changed."

The leader motioned to the driver, who, along with the man from the backseat, was now standing behind Pedro. They both had guns pointed at his back. They pushed Pedro to walk around the car, eventually standing next to Ortiz.

"I feel like you need to be taught a lesson," the leader said.

"Please, you have my daughter, you have my money. What else do you want?"

"I don't feel like I have your respect yet."

"You do. You have it. I just want my family back. I have done everything you have asked."

"I feel like we need to teach you a lesson. We need to show you that we're not the kind of people you want to mess with."

"What else do you want me to do?" Ortiz asked.

The leader then motioned to the driver, who pointed the gun at the back of Pedro's head and pulled the trigger. Pedro instantly dropped to the ground. Ortiz' body jumped, his eyes almost bulging out of his head as he looked down at Pedro's dead body.

The leader also looked down at Pedro's body, though he didn't seem to have much sympathy for him. He turned his attention back to Ortiz.

"That's what we can do to your daughter. Or maybe even your wife. Or your ex-wife. Or your son. Or even you." The man sighed, then shook his head as he looked at Ortiz. "You shouldn't have ignored those messages."

Ortiz glanced down at Pedro before looking back at the man in front of him. Ortiz seemed like he was in shock. The leader playfully slapped Ortiz on the side of his cheek.

"You're gonna be a good boy and get us the rest of that money, right?"

Ortiz gulped and nervously nodded. There was nothing else he could say.

"Tomorrow," the leader said. "We'll call you again when we're ready. You make sure you have the money. If not, someone else is gonna be lying here next to your friend. You understand?"

Ortiz nodded. "I understand."

The leader nodded to the man from the backseat, who then fired his gun, taking out both front tires. He then went to the back tires and put bullet holes in each of them.

The leader then put his hand out. "Your phone."

Ortiz complied, handing his phone over. The man tossed it on the ground and then pointed his gun at it, blowing a hole right through it.

He looked down at Ortiz' feet. "Hope those shoes are comfortable. Looks like you'll be walking a while."

The leader turned his back to Ortiz and started walking back to the van. They weren't done with Ortiz yet, though. To Ortiz' surprise, one of them delivered a punch to the side of his face, knocking him back to the ground. Then both men started pummeling him, hitting him with punches and kicks. The beating went on for a couple of minutes, until the leader whistled, calling the two men off Ortiz.

With the leader back at the van, he looked over at Ortiz' beaten body, wanting to give him a final message.

"Remember, do what we want, or you can look at your friend there. Someone else from your family will be joining him. That's a promise."

18

Angelina was pacing around the pool. She kept looking at the time, assuming something had gone wrong. It'd been three hours since Ortiz had left. He should have checked in by now. Even if it was to say something went wrong. He should have called. Unless he was dead.

"Why hasn't he called?"

Thrower was trying his best to keep her calm. "It could be that it took longer to get to the meeting spot."

"Three hours?"

"Well, if they led him along for an hour, then it took another hour to get there, or maybe there was some complication."

"A complication like maybe he's dead?"

Thrower shook his head. "No, I'm sure he's fine. He'll call."

"Why hasn't he already? It's taking too long. Something went wrong. I can feel it."

Thrower really couldn't argue that point. He had the feeling that something was amiss as well. He just didn't want to voice it. She had enough to worry about without him adding on to it.

"You feel it too, don't you?"

"There could be any number of reasons he hasn't checked in yet," Thrower replied.

"If he had Rosa, he'd call and tell me she was safe. He wouldn't keep me in the dark."

"Like I said, there could be other reasons he hasn't called yet. Maybe he dropped his phone."

Angelina gave him a glance, like she couldn't believe he'd actually said that. She knew something had gone wrong. Nobody could make her believe otherwise.

Thrower did his best to keep her calm, but he didn't want to lie and tell her everything was good if he thought there was a chance it wasn't. And right now, that chance was extremely high. The fact that Ortiz hadn't yet called was very troubling. That meant something had gone wrong. Ortiz was either dead, or kidnapped as well, or he was tied up somewhere to allow the kidnappers more time to get away from wherever he was.

Another hour went by. There was still no word from Ortiz. Angelina had stopped her pacing and rejoined Thrower at the table. She put her head down, worried that they would soon hear the worst.

They all perked their heads when an alert came up on Eva's phone. She was sitting at the edge of the pool, with just her legs in the water. She quickly went over to the phone, which was lying on the ground. They eagerly waited to hear what it was.

"It's the gate," Eva said. "It was just unlocked. It must be Manuel."

"Wait, you get an alert when the gate opens?" Thrower asked, thinking he might have stumbled upon something. "Did you get that last night?"

Eva shook her head. "No. Only when the code is punched in from the outside. It's just a security feature to make sure nobody else has a code that they put in. There's no alert if it opens from the inside."

Thrower nodded, his hopes for a lead dashed. Angelina sprung up from her seat and ran through the yard before going inside and racing through the house. Thrower quickly followed her, with Eva and Angelina's son following him. They got to the front door just as a car was pulling up to the house. Angelina's heart quickly sank when she noticed it was Espinoza's car. There was obviously some sort of problem, since that wasn't the car they'd left in, and Espinoza wasn't initially with them. And Ortiz had a tendency of calling Espinoza when he needed help with something.

Angelina put her hands over her mouth as she

waited for the car to stop. She prayed that when the doors opened, her daughter would jump out and run to her. Thrower made sure he stayed close to her, just in case she got the unthinkable news that her daughter wasn't coming home. He positioned his body so it was facing her. She wouldn't have been the first person that he caught while they fainted.

The front doors of the vehicle opened, and Ortiz and Espinoza stepped out. It didn't take long for the crowd in front of the house to figure out what was going on. Ortiz' long face told the story. There was a mix of anger and dejection on his face as he closed the door. Angelina started screaming, automatically assuming the worst. Thrower put his arms around her, as her legs started to buckle, holding her up and keeping her on her feet.

"You didn't get her?" Eva asked.

Ortiz sighed and threw his arms up. "No. Not yet."

"What do you mean, not yet?"

"I went to the spot, and she wasn't there. They say she's still safe for now."

Upon hearing that her daughter was still alive, Angelina was able to stop her tears from flowing. She tapped Thrower on the hands. "I'm OK. Thank you." Thrower let her go, seeing that her mood had picked up a little, and she turned back to face her ex-husband. "Where is she?"

"They want another payment tomorrow," Ortiz said.

A frown came over Thrower's face as he looked down at the ground. He knew where this was going. The kidnappers were going to just keep stringing Ortiz along, getting multiple payments, keeping his hopes alive, and he'd likely never get his daughter back safely. He'd seen it before.

"I talked to her," Ortiz said. "I heard her voice. She is alive."

"Why are they doing this?" Angelina asked.

Eva went over to her husband and put her hands on his face. "What happened to you?"

Ortiz put his fingers on a few of the cuts that he now felt. "They gave me a going away present. And a warning at the same time."

Thrower looked past the others and at the car. There was one person missing. "Where is Pedro?"

Ortiz looked down and shook his head. "Pedro is dead."

"What?" Angelina asked. "How?"

"They shot him. They killed him." Ortiz rubbed his face, struggling to get the image of Pedro's bloody body out of his head. "It was terrible. We were standing together and they came up behind him and they just shot him. No provocation. They just executed him."

Eva put her arms around him. "Let's go inside so you can sit down."

Everyone went inside, with Eva getting her husband a drink, as the others sat down.

"So what happened out there?" Thrower asked.

Ortiz' head moved around, as if he was trying to remember everything. "After we left here, we drove around for a while. They kept sending us to different spots. Eventually we stopped on the side of the road, and a man got in the back seat. Um, I don't remember if it was before or after that, but at one point, I asked to speak to Rosa. I said I wasn't going anywhere unless I knew she was still alive."

"And you spoke to her?"

"Yes," Ortiz replied. "It was her voice."

"You're sure? It wasn't the voice of some other child that was similar to hers, or maybe you just wanted to believe it was hers?"

"No, it was her," Ortiz answered. "I swear it. It was her. There is no doubt in my mind."

"OK, that's good," Thrower said. "What else?"

"We then drove around a bit more, then went to this meeting place. We got there, got out, then the white van drove up. Two men got out, I gave them the money, and then they said it wasn't enough. That they wanted another payment tomorrow. Same amount."

"What about Pedro?" Thrower asked.

"They brought us both together, and then they just shot him. He didn't do anything. We were just standing there and one of them shot him in the back of the head. Then they started working me over. They smashed my phone, beat me up, and shot all of my tires, so I had to walk for a while. I eventually came across a store, and they let me use a phone to call Carlos."

"What about this payment tomorrow? They say anything else about it?"

Ortiz shook his head. "No. They just said they would be in touch. To take more money out of the bank, and they'll call me later. Today, tomorrow, I don't know. I don't know." He put his hands over his face. "Maybe they said, I'm not sure. It's all very blurry right now."

"We should have had Nate go," Angelina said. "We made a mistake in keeping him here."

Ortiz put his hand up. "Maybe so. But they didn't even bring Rosa anyway, so what good would it have done? He might be dead now too."

"No use worrying about what's done and over with," Thrower said. "All we can do now is go from here. From now on, wherever you go, I have to have eyes on you. Somehow, someway, I need to be watching. Whatever it takes."

Ortiz nodded. "Agreed."

"What about these guys? Did they say anything else? They give a reason as to why they're targeting you?"

Ortiz scrunched his face together like he was trying to remember. "Uh, yes, yes. The one guy, he seemed to be in charge, he said something about..." He put his hands on his forehead as he struggled to think of the words. "What did he say?"

"Just take your time," Thrower said. "Everything's still fresh. Relax. Think."

Ortiz took a deep breath. "He said something about me not remembering him. That I never noticed anyone unless it made me money, or something to that effect. And that even people that made me money, I still didn't notice them. And he said that hasn't changed."

"So it's obviously someone you've known at some point."

Ortiz started shaking his head. "But I don't recognize him. He did not look familiar to me at all."

"What about his voice?" Thrower asked. "You remember that?"

Ortiz continued to shake his head rather quickly. "No, I don't. His face, his voice, his movements, none of it is familiar. I don't remember him. I don't know what he thinks I did to him."

"Could be from when you were just starting your business? Building it up? Maybe you stepped on a few toes?"

Ortiz wiped his face with both hands, obviously frustrated. "I don't know. I just don't know."

"Well, that doesn't really matter right now anyway," Thrower said. "Why takes a back seat to figuring out where they are."

"If we make another payment tomorrow, do you think they would finally let Rosa go?" Angelina asked.

"I wouldn't count on it," Thrower said. "The longer this goes on, the worse her chances are. I'm sure they don't want to be taking care of a kid for days or weeks, or even longer. A kid can only slow them down. They don't want to keep her any more than you want them to have her."

"So why not let her go today?"

"Because they figure they can get more money. Speaking of which, do you have another payment to give them?"

Ortiz nodded. "Yes, there is more. But what is the point? As you said, if they didn't give her back today, what makes us believe they would do it tomorrow?"

"They probably wouldn't," Thrower replied. "That means by that time we gotta find her, get her, and bring her back."

"But how? How can we do that? We have nothing on them."

Thrower's phone then rang. He looked at the ID. It was Jones. "Nothing yet. Maybe that's about to change."

19

Thrower stepped outside, closing the door behind him, letting the others continue to talk about what had happened with Ortiz. He answered his phone as he walked around the pool.

"David, hope you've got something for me."

"Indeed I do," Jones replied. "I have been able to pick up the van in question through several surveillance cameras that I was able to dig into."

"Great. Were you able to get a location?"

"I'm trying to pinpoint the exact location now. I'm pretty sure I've got the area pinned down. Just trying to get the specific spot for you."

"I'd really appreciate it if you could," Thrower said. "Things are getting out of control quickly here."

"Why, what happened?"

Thrower relayed what had happened with Ortiz and the kidnappers. "Feels like things are spiraling."

"So it appears. It sounds as if you could use some help."

"Like I said before, I don't want to drag you guys away from your thing."

"Nonsense. You've helped us. The least we can do is return the favor. I've already appraised Mike and Chris of the situation. They're both willing to help, though I figure it'll be best if one of them stays here, just in case something breaks."

"Definitely a good idea," Thrower said. "You're sure they wanna come down?"

Jones was sitting at his desk, then looked over at the door as he heard Recker come in. "Hold on a second." Jones held the phone up, handing it off to Recker as he walked over.

"Nate, how's it going?" Recker asked.

"Things have been better," Thrower answered.

"Yeah, I've heard you've got some problems down there."

"That's not even the half of it." Thrower then went over the situation with Ortiz and the kidnappers again.

"Wow. Sounds like things are really heating up there."

"Yeah."

"I can be there in the morning."

"You sure?" Thrower asked. "Is Mia going to be OK with you just picking up and leaving for another country just like that?"

"Mia's working a double starting in the morning.

So by the time she gets home, goes to sleep, wakes up, it'll be a couple of days anyway. Besides, this shouldn't take too long, right?"

"I don't know about that. I don't know of a location on these guys yet. Still waiting on David to pin it down."

"He'll hopefully get it soon," Recker said.

"There's another meeting probably going down tomorrow, so if we don't get it today, tomorrow's gonna get dicey again."

"Either way, we'll be covered."

"How you figure?"

"If I get there in the morning before any of this goes down, you and I might have time to hit their hideout, before the meeting starts."

"And if we can't?" Thrower asked.

"Well, it should still work out in our favor."

"How you mean?"

"Your client will need a new bodyguard to accompany him to the meeting, right? Someone that's not you?"

"Yeah?"

Recker smiled as he said it. "Looks like he might have one."

"It'll be dangerous. They've killed one person already."

Recker laughed. "Well, we'll just have to make sure it ends with that. At least on our end. Their end... not so much."

"You're sure I'm not taking you away from anything important there?"

"No. We just finished something up. David says nothing else is imminent. You know I don't like to go too long between projects. I start to get antsy."

"So I've heard," Thrower said. "OK, well, I appreciate the help. I guess I'll see you tomorrow morning at some point."

"Yeah. Just send me the address of where you want to meet, and I'll be there."

"Probably just be easier to meet here at Ortiz' house and go from there. I'll send you the address, though."

"Sounds good. See you tomorrow."

Thrower hung up and looked at the pool as he put the phone back in his pocket. He certainly felt better about the situation having Recker come down to help. But that was tomorrow. They still had to get through today. And who could tell if the rest of this day would go by without incident? What if the kidnappers called back with some other demand? He'd just have to deal with things as they came, if they came at all. He hoped, though, that they could spend the rest of the day trying to prepare themselves for tomorrow. It would come soon enough.

Thrower went back inside the house, finding the others in the same position as when he'd left. Nobody was talking, though. They all looked depressed and despondent. It was understandable. With the loss of

Pedro and Rosa still missing, there wasn't much to feel hopeful about. Thrower hoped that would change soon.

"Looks like I've got some help coming down."

Ortiz' head perked. "Who?"

"Guy named Mike. He's a friend of mine. He'll be here in the morning."

"What good will that do?" Angelina asked.

"If the demands tomorrow are the same as today, and they still want me to stay away, Manuel will need a new bodyguard."

"You saw what happened today with Pedro," Ortiz said.

"With all due respect to Pedro, this isn't an apples-to-apples comparison. Mike does this type of stuff for a living, too."

"What are you suggesting? That when the meeting happens tomorrow, that your friend will take out all the kidnappers?"

Thrower shrugged. It wasn't necessarily what he was implying, though it certainly was a distinct possibility. If things did go down in that manner, there was no doubt that Thrower believed Recker would handle it better. But it was also very possible that it wouldn't come down to that. Besides being able to handle himself if bullets started flying, Recker also knew how to talk and negotiate in these types of matters. Even if it was only to buy himself more time and get himself into a more advantageous position. In any case, Thrower had more confidence in Recker if the situation deteriorated.

"I'm suggesting that Mike will be able to handle whatever the situation calls for," Thrower said. "If it's a shootout, if it's just a negotiation, whatever it is, he'll know what to do. And right now, without me being there, that's what we need."

"Does he know of what happened to Pedro today?"

"He knows."

"And he's still willing to put himself in that position?"

"He's not worried."

Ortiz shook his head and wiped his forehead. "I don't know how you people can act so calmly in situations like this."

"Training and experience."

"I don't even know if I can go through with it again."

"Manuel, you have to," Angelina said. "For Rosa."

Ortiz looked at his ex-wife and sighed, nodding that he agreed. Reliving that situation again wasn't something that he looked forward to. No normal person should. It was a terrifying ordeal that he wished he wouldn't have to repeat. But he would have to. For the safety of his daughter.

"Do you think they will do the same thing tomorrow as they did today?" Ortiz asked.

"What, you mean the whole driving around thing?"

Thrower replied. "Then taking you to some remote location?"

"Yes."

"Worked today. No reason to think they might change their plans."

"And what makes you think the result will be any different?"

"Like I said, if things go down, I have confidence that Mike will be able to handle it. Plus, I'm not sitting on the sidelines."

"But what else can we do?" Ortiz asked. "If they do not want you to be there, how can you be?"

"I'd have to coordinate something with Mike. Something that will allow me to know where he is without following too closely, and therefore drawing the kidnappers' attention. We can figure it out. But one thing's for sure: I'm not sitting here again. That didn't work. Now we'll do it my way."

"Whatever you think is best."

"I can't believe this nightmare is happening," Angelina said. "I just want my baby back."

Thrower walked over and put his hand on her shoulder. "And you'll get her. We'll get her."

"I guess I should go to the bank and get the money?" Ortiz asked.

"Not yet. Let's wait until later in the day."

"What for?"

"Because they were watching there the first time,"

Thrower answered. "We have to assume they'd be watching there again."

"So? What difference does waiting make?"

"Because last time they called as soon as you walked out. And they upped the meeting time. What if they decide to do that again?"

Ortiz nodded, now understanding what his bodyguard was saying. "So we want to delay that as long as possible to allow enough time for your friend to get here."

"Exactly."

"But if that's the case, then, what if they call later?"

Thrower shook his head. "They said tomorrow for the next meeting. There's no use in helping them up the time frame. Wait until tomorrow to take out the rest of the money."

"As you wish."

"Do you really believe your friend will be able to help?" Angelina asked.

"I do," Thrower replied.

"But there will still only be two of you."

Thrower tried to give her a comforting smile. "I like our chances."

"But what if they don't bring Rosa tomorrow, either?"

"All we can do is take it one step at a time. The first step is getting there. The next step after that will depend on them."

"What if you have overestimated your friend's abilities?" Ortiz asked. "What if he cannot handle them, either?"

Thrower shook his head. "No, you don't know him like I do. I've worked with him before. He knows his stuff. If there's a problem, he knows how to squash it. They don't call him the Silencer for nothing."

20

A few hours went by. Everyone else was outside by the pool, as usual. Thrower went to his room, spending some time on his laptop. He was going through some satellite photos of the area, including where Ortiz had met the kidnappers, hoping something would stick out to him. It was mostly just busy work, though. He just needed to stay busy.

He didn't want to keep thinking about the meeting tomorrow, especially since he didn't know what it would entail yet. It could've been the exact same setup, or they might try something different. There was no use in speculating until he knew what the deal would be.

There was a knock on the door.

"It's open," Thrower said.

The door opened, with Eva standing there in her bikini, holding a drink. "I thought you could use this."

Thrower grabbed the glass and took a whiff of it. Whatever it was, it smelled strong. "What is it?"

"Enough to make you relax. I figured you've been stressed out enough with all this."

Thrower took a sip. He was right with his initial impression. It was strong. He put it down on the end table. "Thanks. I'll finish it in a bit."

Eva sat down on the bed next to him. She leaned in closer to him, looking at his laptop. "What are you doing?"

"I dunno. Just looking at things."

"Oh. Anything you like?"

It was the way she said it that perked his ears. It didn't sound the way it should in a normal conversation. It sounded somewhat flirty. Then he felt her hand on his knee. He looked down, seeing her hand slowly work up his leg to his thigh. She then leaned over and kissed him on the cheek.

Thrower instantly got up. "This is not gonna work."

Eva leaned back on the bed, puffing her chest out, letting one of the straps on her bikini top fall down past her shoulder. She then pulled down the other strap and pulled down on her top, exposing her breasts.

"Do you not like what you see?"

Thrower looked at her body and cleared his throat. There wasn't anything not to like. Except for the fact that she was married and throwing herself at him.

"Yes, but, uh, you're married."

"Manuel and I love each other. But we met while he was cheating on his then wife. And I'm sure he has done it since we have been married, too. Have you seen some of his secretaries and other people who work there? They haven't all gotten their positions because of their talents. Well, their work talents, anyway."

"And that doesn't bother you?" Thrower asked.

"I'm the one he comes home to at night. If he wants to have an occasional fling on the side, it's fine."

Thrower raised his brows. He was aware that some couples had these types of relationships, though he believed this was the first one he'd seen up close and personal. At least that he knew of.

"Besides, it's not like I let him have all the fun while I'm stuck at home doing laundry."

"Meaning?" Thrower asked.

"If I go out and about and I see something I like, I have my fun too." The way she said it, Thrower could tell she meant it in the most seductive and flirty way possible.

"So you're both stepping out on each other, and you're both fine with it?"

"Of course. It's just sex. Like I said, I'm the one who he comes home to. And he's the one I come back to. Everything works."

"Interesting."

"You see? It's fine. Just let your inhibitions go." She puffed her chest out a little further, hoping to finally get him to make a move.

Eva stuck her hands out, wanting Thrower to grab them. After standing there and considering it for a second, he relented and took her hands. She pulled him closer, with his six-four frame straddling overtop of her as she laid back on the bed. Thrower lowered his head, their lips just about touching.

"You're a beautiful woman."

"Just kiss me."

Their lips barely touched before Thrower pulled his head back up. "But you're still married."

"What?"

Thrower reached over and grabbed her bikini top, bringing it over and laying it on top of her chest. "It may work for you, but it's not how I do things."

Eva looked incredulous. "Are you serious? You're going to do nothing? I'm lying here half-naked, and you can do what you want to me, and you refuse?"

Thrower grinned, then playfully tapped her on the cheek. "That's about the size of it."

He then got up and left the room, leaving Eva still lying on the bed, though he never looked back to see if she was getting dressed or not. Thrower went back outside, where the rest of the family, including Espinoza, was still gathered. Ortiz, along with his son, was in the pool, probably waiting for Eva to come back. Espinoza was sitting by himself in a lounge chair, a laptop across his legs. Angelina was sitting alone at a table.

Angelina watched Thrower as he came outside,

then noticed Eva come back out not too long after that. She watched each of them closely. Thrower eventually came over to her table.

"Mind if I join you?" Thrower asked.

Angelina smiled and held her hand out. "Please."

Though Thrower wasn't looking at her, she studied his face for a few moments. He was looking away, appearing as though he had something on his mind. He sighed and kept looking up at the sky. She then glanced back at Eva, whose face looked a little more sorrowful than it did just a few minutes ago.

"Did she come on to you?"

Thrower scrunched his cheeks. "What?"

"Eva. She went inside, a pleasant look on her face, a smile on her lips. Now she looks like someone gave her bad news."

Thrower shook his head. "I wouldn't know."

Angelina laughed. "You are a good man."

"Think so?"

"I've seen the way she looks at you when you're in the same room. She is interested in you."

Thrower shrugged. "Like I said, I wouldn't know."

"Did she flirt with you, offer her body, and you turned her down?"

"Now is really not the time for that type of stuff."

"I agree. That is why you're a good man. Most men wouldn't resist her. She's pretty, has a good body, and she's not afraid to show it."

Thrower looked over at Eva, who was now in the

The Bodyguard

pool. He couldn't deny any of those things. "I suppose not."

"So why did you resist her?"

Thrower chuckled. "Is this really what you wanna talk about right now?"

"I guess thinking of other things that aren't really important is keeping my mind off of Rosa."

Thrower nodded, understanding her point. With that being the case, he was willing to do his part in helping her.

"So am I correct?" Angelina asked.

It was still a little difficult for Thrower to admit. He wasn't in the habit of dishing about personal details like that. "Maybe."

Angelina grinned. "So why did you say no? I doubt many men would have joined you in that response."

"Maybe not. But I'm not like most people."

"That I can see. If my husband was more like you, we might still be together."

"I don't know about that. And it's ex-husband, as I'm often reminded. But you know, if it wasn't Eva, it most likely would have been someone else."

"Yes, I know. I have often thought of that over the years."

"Is she the one you're really mad at?" Thrower asked.

"No. I mean, sometimes I make it sound that way, but you're right. If it's in a man's heart to wander, he will wander, regardless of the circumstances."

"Do you still hold out some hope for a reconciliation?"

Angelina shook her head as she looked at the pool. "No, I think the time for that has long since passed. But back to you and Eva."

Thrower laughed. "There is no me and Eva."

"Why not? Is there a Mrs. Thrower somewhere?"

Thrower smiled to keep himself from laughing again. "No. No missus out there."

"Why not?"

"I don't think this is the kind of life to have someone waiting for me. Waiting and worrying. That's no life for anybody."

"And I'm sure a big, strong, attractive man like yourself has his share of women."

"Probably not as many as you think."

"Waiting for that... beach house. Right?"

Thrower grinned. "That's right."

"Be honest. Are you really saving up for a beach house for retirement?"

"Of course. Why else?"

"Seems to me like a man like you, who's well-thought of and gets a good payment for these kinds of jobs, would be well on his way to that beach house by now."

"What, you think I'm sticking around just to put myself in harm's way if I didn't have to?"

Angelina tapped her fingers on the table. "I'm not

sure. I have a feeling that you have other things that drive you besides money and beach houses."

"Such as?"

"Things like fairness, loyalty, sense of duty, pride, things like that. Maybe the thought that you actually make a difference. Maybe that's what keeps you on this path."

The corner of Thrower's lips raised slightly, indicating that maybe she had hit on something, not that he was likely to admit it, though. He was about to respond, but then his phone rang, letting him off the hook. He eagerly pulled his phone out of his pocket to see who it was. It was Jones. Thrower hoped that his friend had found something. Either that, or he was calling with bad news. Hopefully that wouldn't be the case, but Thrower had to brace himself for the possibility.

"Is this good or bad news?"

"That is yet to be determined," Jones replied.

"I don't like the sound of that."

"Most things in our business could be good or bad at first sight. It's what happens when we get the information afterwards that determines which way it goes."

"Can't really argue that," Thrower said. "So what do you have?"

"I'd like to show you. Do you have a computer nearby? That way I can share my screen with you and we can go over it."

"It's inside. I'll go get it."

Thrower got up and walked around the pool, going inside the house. He went to his room and closed the door. He sat down on the bed and opened his laptop, turning it on.

"I'm going to email you a link so we can both look at the same thing," Jones said.

Thrower logged onto his email address, and saw Jones' name. He clicked on the link, sending him to a website that he wasn't familiar with. But he saw Jones' smiling face, waving at him.

Thrower took the phone away from his ear and looked at it before putting it down. "Guess I don't need that anymore, huh?"

"I would say not."

Jones' and Thrower's face was on the left of the screen, while Jones started bringing up other videos to the right of them.

"What am I looking at?" Thrower asked.

Jones continued typing. "There we go. A picture of the van in question should be coming up on screen now."

Thrower saw a white van driving. "That looks like it's it."

"This was a video taken only a few minutes away from the house last night around the time you told me."

"Yeah, I think that's it."

"I'm gonna play the video, at least what I have of it.

I've edited a bunch of videos together to make it continuous."

"Do we know where it went after that?" Thrower asked.

"I'm getting to that." Jones fast-forwarded the video, getting to the end of it. They both kept watching as it played. "This is where I lose it. It turns onto this street here."

"Are there no other cameras nearby?"

"That's the thing. There are. So the fact that I haven't seen it again must mean that it's still on that street somewhere."

"So it turned onto that street and hasn't come out," Thrower said.

"Correct."

"You're sure it couldn't have slipped out somewhere?"

"Well, I've looked at all the maps, and according to my calculations, if it left that street again, I would have seen it on either end. I've triple-checked the cameras, and unless they stripped it apart and put it back together again as a sedan and painted it a different color, it hasn't left."

"What's on that street?"

Jones pulled up various images of the street in question, mostly from satellite photos or from the internet. "Just looks like a regular street of homes. Maybe a small business or two on the ends."

"So Rosa should be there."

"I can't say. There is the possibility that they just ditched the van there and had another vehicle waiting."

"That doesn't seem likely," Thrower replied. "I mean, they've been driving around in that thing on several occasions when I've run into them."

"Or maybe they were just using it until they grabbed the girl. I don't know. It's just food for thought."

"Were you able to get a good look at the driver or passenger?"

"No," Jones answered. "Nothing that I could run through a facial scan or anything. Just blurred images, mostly. Which also means that I can't definitively rule out that they left in another car because I was not able to see their faces."

"Were there other cars that left after the van pulled in?"

"Yes, there were several. But like I said, I can't definitively say they were or were not in any of them."

"Well, looks like it's something to work with, anyway."

"It definitely is."

"Now I got a decision to make," Thrower said.

"Which is?"

"Do I go pursue this on my own and see if I can find the girl and take her back? Or do I just wait until tomorrow when Mike gets here and continue with the meeting as planned?"

"What does your gut say?" Jones asked.

"My gut says I should check this out now. What if Rosa's alive, but they decide they don't need her by the time tomorrow comes?"

Jones nodded. "That is a possibility, yes. One that can't be discounted."

"That would also mean I leave the rest of them unprotected as I investigate this."

"I think that is a tradeoff they would take, if it meant bringing their daughter back safely."

"Probably so. It's not without risks, though. What if I get there and I engage with them, and I still can't get her? What then? Does that make them angrier? Does that put Rosa's life in jeopardy even more than it is? Do they change the deal further? Make it worse?"

"Those are a lot of questions, Nathan. A lot of good questions. I'm afraid none of us have the answers to them. All we can do is speculate. And weigh the risks. Then live with the consequences, however it turns out. Can you not get anyone else there for backup?"

Thrower shook his head. "Can't afford to take any chances. There were two guards. One's dead, and the other's in the wind. I can't afford to bring in someone else I don't know. Can't trust them."

"I understand. Well, the choice is yours on how to proceed from here. I can continue digging to see if I can come up with anything else, but I don't think I'm going to have much luck, to be honest. So it's likely that's all there is."

"It's better than nothing and a lot more than what I had."

"Wish I could gift wrap it for you, but it's just not feasible, I'm afraid."

Thrower cleared his throat, then turned his head away as he put his hand over his mouth, thinking about his options. "I have to go over there. I don't think I can wait."

"I understand."

"If we go to the meeting and find out something happened that I could've prevented if I'd just acted sooner, I don't know what I'd do."

Jones smiled. It sounded familiar to him. "It's what Mike would do as well. You have to act on the information you have at the moment. You can't worry about what ifs and maybes if you can prevent anything else from happening."

"Can you text me the location once we get off here?"

"I certainly will. And let me know as soon as the situation is resolved. Well, hopefully resolved. If you take care of it today, then Mike can cancel his trip down there. And if not, then we'll proceed as previously scheduled."

"I will. Either way, I'll let you know how it goes. Hopefully, I'll find Rosa and we don't have to worry about tomorrow. And if I find those other guys, may God help them."

21

As soon as Thrower got off the call with Jones, he went under his bed and pulled out his backpack. He usually kept a few weapons in there, as well as some ammo, mostly that he used for backup purposes. He slung it over his shoulder and walked outside again. This time, everyone was out of the pool. Surprisingly enough, Ortiz, Angelina, Eva, and Espinoza were all sitting at the same table. Times like this were enough to bring anybody together, Thrower thought.

They all turned and looked at Thrower as he approached. They saw the backpack on his shoulder and assumed something was up. He was also walking with a purpose.

"That call," Angelina said. "Was it your friend?"

"Yes," Thrower answered. "He thinks he has something."

"What?" Ortiz said. "He found Rosa?"

"No, not directly. He's got a general area he thinks the van parked their car. Well, a street, to be exact."

"He knows where they are?"

"Not the exact building," Thrower replied. "He found the van on a surveillance camera turning on one street. He never saw it leave."

"Then Rosa must be there."

"Maybe."

"Are you going to find her?" Angelina asked.

"I'm going to try," Thrower said. "I can't make any promises. Maybe the kidnappers just ditched the van there and had another car waiting. Maybe they're in some house or room there. And maybe it's just a dead end."

"Or maybe she's there."

Thrower nodded. "Or maybe she's there. But if I go check this out, it presents another problem."

"Which is?"

"There's nobody here to protect you if I leave."

"They wouldn't try to attack us again here, would they?" Ortiz asked. "I mean, why would they? They already have our daughter. They already have some of my money. What else could they want?"

Thrower shrugged. "I'm just presenting the possibilities. Even if they're remote. Maybe they come for your other child. Or your wife. Or ex-wife. Or you. Or they just want to be done with all of this and want to kill you all. I don't know. Maybe none of those things are likely. But I wouldn't be doing my job if I didn't tell you the risks."

"I don't suppose we could actually come with you?" Angelina asked.

"Absolutely not. I can't be focused on finding Rosa or the kidnappers if I'm worried about protecting you guys too. It can only be me."

"Then you have to go. We will be fine here. Do not worry about us."

Ortiz agreed. "Yes. We can take care of ourselves. If you can find Rosa and bring her back, that is all that matters."

Thrower put the backpack down on the ground and opened it. "Good. In saying that, I'd still feel better if I knew I left you something to help, just in case something happens."

"Like what?"

Thrower pulled out a couple of pistols. "Like these." He handed one to Ortiz and one to Angelina. "Protect yourselves at all costs if something happens."

Angelina looked at the gun and held it in her hand, like it was going to bite her. "I don't know if I can do this."

"Have either of you ever fired a gun before?"

They both shook their heads. Thrower then looked at Eva and Espinoza. Neither of them had either. Thrower sighed, but understood not everyone was as proficient with firearms as he was. He spent the next several minutes teaching them what they had to do in the unlikely event they actually had to use the weapons. And so they wouldn't blow their own foot off. Once they had a basic understanding, Thrower figured that was good enough. They didn't need to be sharpshooters. They really didn't even need to know anything other than how to safely handle the gun.

"And if we actually have to use these?" Ortiz asked.

"If you actually shoot that, you aim right here." Thrower pointed to the middle of his chest. "You fire three rounds right here. And that should stop anybody."

"What if we just shoot them in the leg or the shoulder?"

"If you try to shoot them in the leg or the shoulder, first of all, you'll probably miss. Second of all, even if you connect with that, they'll probably still kill you. Remember that. A wounded man is a dangerous man. Always. If you're gonna shoot that thing, you shoot to kill. No good person wants to kill anybody. But if you have to defend yourself or your family, you do what's gotta be done. Understand?"

Ortiz nodded. "Perfectly. We'll do it."

"Good. Now in saying that, hopefully you have a peaceful few hours until I get back."

"I will pray that you bring Rosa back," Angelina said.

"Good," Thrower replied. "We'll probably need it."

Once Thrower got to the vicinity of the street that Jones told him about, he parked a couple of streets away. He knew it could be a challenge getting out, as it would be a longer distance to cover, especially if they were dodging bullets while they were trying to escape. But the main thing was getting in by surprise. If he could do that, that was the most important objective. He'd just have to take his chances that he could outrun them if they were in pursuit. Of course, finding them would be the biggest challenge.

The only thing he really had going for him was that it was nighttime. With the night as his ally, Thrower also put on a baseball cap and a baggy shirt. With his big, muscular frame, it did make him stand out sometimes. It also could make him easier to identify if someone was looking for him. He had to try to hide that. A hat pulled down low and a baggier shirt to hide some of his muscles sometimes did the trick. He just had to hope it did the trick this time.

As Thrower walked along a sidewalk, he passed a few people, but there weren't that many out. Once he got to the street in question, he turned to his right and surveyed the area. It still looked the same as it did in the pictures that Jones had sent him. To his left, there was a row of buildings, mostly houses attached to each other, though the building on the end looked like some kind of convenience store. There were ten buildings, nine of them seeming to be residential houses.

Thrower looked to his immediate right and was

happy to see that there was nothing there. Nothing in terms of occupied buildings, that is. There was a tall chain-link fence, probably eight or ten feet high, with lots of trees and bushes lined up against it. On the other side of the fence was a manufacturing plant, though it had closed many years before that. Still, it looked to be a perfect spot to set up shop for a few hours and do some surveillance.

Thrower walked along the street, keeping his head down, putting his hand along the fence as he walked. He only barely looked up, trying to see out of the corner of his eye, though it wasn't working as well as he'd hoped. The buildings were all two-stories, so he wasn't getting as good a view as he wanted, but he also didn't want to give the appearance that he was looking for something in particular. He was trying to blend.

The few times he did look up, Thrower didn't see anything of interest. As he continued to walk, he noticed a couple of small holes in the fence toward the bottom. It looked like holes that people had crawled through to get inside the property. Most likely kids or criminals doing the usual things. In either case, it seemed to be good enough to suit his purposes.

There were cars lined up against the side of the street that he was walking as far down as he could see. Thrower tried to spot the van, but there were several other cars and trucks in the way. As he got three-quarters of the way down the street, he saw it. The same white van that he was familiar with. Parked along the curb nestled in between a couple of other cars.

Thrower slowed down as he got to the van, though he didn't stop. If someone was watching from a window, they might take notice of his interest in the vehicle. Walking slower, Thrower carefully looked the van over, at least the side he could see. That was it, though. It still had the dirt spots on it. There was no question it was the same vehicle. Plus, it was the only white van there.

Though it was nice to confirm the van was still there, it really didn't erase any of the questions that Thrower had going through his mind. It didn't mean the kidnappers were there. And if they were, it didn't tell him which building they were in. And what if they just parked there, then went on to another street?

As Thrower walked to the end of the street, he noticed more holes in the fence. What if the kidnappers used that to escape from the view of the cameras at both ends of the street? That could be why Jones never saw them leave. The holes were probably big enough for adults to crawl through. Maybe they were in that big, empty manufacturing building.

Thrower walked to the end of the street, then turned a corner. There was still that same fence that went around on his right side, complete with the periodic holes in it. Once Thrower walked a few more feet, he stopped. He leaned up against the fence, trying to look casual, like he was doing nothing more than just hanging out.

With nobody walking or looking on that he could see, Thrower quickly dropped to the ground and crawled through one of the holes. Now on the inside part of the fence, he quickly stayed close to the trees and bushes, knowing it provided some cover for him.

The actual manufacturing building was a good distance away, and there was a lot of open space between where Thrower currently was and the main building. Too much space for Thrower's liking. If that's where the kidnappers were, they would likely see him long before he got to the building. And that's if he ever actually got to the building. If those guys were good shots, Thrower wouldn't stand a chance of getting there.

Thrower, still not convinced which direction he should be watching, maneuvered his way to the back fence, where he could still keep an eye on the van and the houses across from it. He could also look back at the manufacturing building, not that he could see a lot from where he was.

Thrower sighed, not liking how much uncertainty there was with all this. It would be hard enough if he knew the actual location, but now having to keep his eyes peeled in several different directions made it almost impossible. He had to practically keep his head on a swivel, or else he would risk missing something.

As Thrower knelt down within the confines of the

foliage, he heard some people walking on the other side of the fence. He kept out of sight and stayed quiet, though he peeked through some leaves with one eye. It was just a couple of friends out walking, it seemed. They were gone within a few seconds.

Thrower kept his gaze shifting in both directions for a few more minutes, though he eventually started keeping his eyes mostly on the residential buildings. The manufacturing place was just too far away to accurately see anything. At least with the homes, he would be able to see people moving by windows, or if someone was peeking outside, or if someone walked to the van and back. He couldn't tell any of those things at the manufacturing plant.

Thrower's eyes scanned the length of the row of buildings, hoping he could pick up something. All he needed was the slightest of clues. Something to point him in the right direction. He didn't get it, though. At least, not yet. It only reinforced to Thrower that it could be a long and frustrating night.

22

Thrower spent the next two hours in the same spot. Kneeling down, nestled in between some bushes, his eyes firmly fixed on the buildings in front of him. Not much had changed in the time he'd been there. He saw and heard a few people walking, but nothing that led him any closer to what he was looking for. And not a single sign of the kidnappers or of Rosa.

At least Thrower had a picture of the kidnappers in his mind. After going up against them several times by now, he wasn't operating blind. He would know them again if he saw them. It was just getting to the seeing part that troubled him.

The good part of being there at that time of night was that there was less of a chance of someone spotting him. He could blend in. The bad part was that there were fewer people out and about, which meant less of a chance of him spotting someone else. He just had to hope he'd get that opportunity to see one of the people he was looking for. Just one. Then he'd know the others weren't far behind.

Unfortunately, his luck didn't change over the next hour. Actually, nothing changed at all. Thrower was starting to think he'd wind up staying there until the sun came up. That would present another host of challenges that he didn't want to think about.

Then, he heard something, and Thrower's head snapped to his left to identify what it was. It sounded like the fence rattling a bit. He then heard a few voices. He tried to remain hidden in the bushes as he looked on to see what was happening.

He saw three men standing there. Well, maybe they were men. It actually looked like one man and a couple of young boys, probably in their late teens. Thrower figured they were eighteen, maybe nineteen. The other guy appeared to be in his thirties or forties.

Thrower tried to understand what they were saying, as they were speaking Spanish. He could pick out a few words. What was more important was what they were doing. It appeared to be some type of drug buy. The older man was passing off a bag to the younger two.

Though Thrower was concerned about the younger two, there was nothing he could do about their activities. And he wasn't in the scaring them straight game. Definitely not now. He had other things on his mind. But maybe these people could tell him something. Maybe they had some information he could use. Especially the older one. Drug sellers usually had a long list of buyers and connections. And they were usually familiar with what went on in a certain neighborhood. Thrower had to assume this guy was no different.

Thrower emerged from the shadows and started walking toward the threesome. With Thrower's frame, he almost always stood out. It was unlikely he'd ever sneak up on anyone, not unless he was able to stay hidden until it was time to strike. That wasn't one of these times.

As Thrower walked toward them, they noticed him coming. They immediately tried to scatter. The two teenagers quickly got to a hole in the fence and climbed through it. Thrower ran after them. Unfortunately for the older guy, he wasn't quite as fast as his younger clients. As he waited for the teenagers to get through the hole, Thrower was able to get his hands on the dealer's shirt. He then nonchalantly flung him backwards.

As the man fell over and rolled onto his back, then to his knees, he put his hands out as Thrower slowly started to approach. He started speaking Spanish, and his face clearly indicated the concern over what he thought was going to happen.

¿Hablas inglés?" Thrower asked.

"Un poco."

"Let's start with what you're doing here."

The Bodyguard

The man let out an uncomfortable laugh. "Just trying to make a living, man. That's all."

"Is that so?"

"You American?"

"All right, enough with the small talk, I don't care about any of that. I need some information."

"I don't know anything," the man said.

"That's the wrong answer, considering I haven't asked anything yet."

Thrower figured this was the type of guy who had to be scared for his life before he said anything. The whole snitches end up in ditches thing. Thrower had to convince the guy he'd wind up in a ditch if he didn't talk. He removed his gun from his waist and let his hand drop to the side of his leg, making sure the man could clearly see it.

"Wait, there's no need for that, right?"

"There is if you don't tell me what I want to know."

"I'm not even armed, man. I'm just a nobody trying to make a living here. That's all."

"Look, there's two ways this can go. You can either tell me what I want to know and then you can get out of here, or you can sit there and play stupid, and I'll put a bullet in your leg."

"You're bluffing."

Thrower pointed his gun at the man's thigh.

The man gulped, closed his eyes, and turned his head away. "No, please don't."

"Are we done with the games?"

"Why? Why are you doing this to me? What'd I do to you?"

"Nothing. I'm looking for a little girl who was taken. Time's running out. And I don't have time to stand here and play games with you."

"So if I tell you what you want to know, you'll let me go?"

Thrower nodded. "I don't give a crap about you. You can go on and do your thing."

"OK. What do you want to know?"

"I want to know about that white van out there." Thrower pointed backwards with his thumb.

"What white van?"

"Well, get up and look."

"You won't shoot me if I get up?"

"Not if you help me."

The man slowly got up, though he hesitated in moving as he looked Thrower over. Thrower looked even larger to the man now that he was standing up. Definitely not someone he wanted to mess with.

"Come on," Thrower said, waving in the direction of the van with his gun.

The dealer started moving toward the hole in the fence to see what the big guy was talking about. Thrower quickly put a stop to that, grabbing him by the shirt and pulling him back.

"Not that way! I don't want people to see you." Thrower then pointed to the bushes. "Over there."

"Oh. Good thinking."

The Bodyguard

Thrower rolled his eyes, then followed the man over to the bushes. The man took a look at the cars in the street, noticing the white van. He pointed to it.

"That one there? That the one?"

"That's the one," Thrower answered.

"Never seen it before, man."

That wasn't the answer Thrower wanted to hear. And he didn't believe it was the truth. He sighed loudly, wanting the man to hear his displeasure. "That's too bad."

Thrower then jammed the gun into the small of the man's back, making sure he felt it. The man just froze as he felt the barrel pressed up against his spine.

"What's going on, man?"

"What'd I tell you about the games?" Thrower replied. He was growing more agitated. "I told you. There is a little girl's life at stake here. I don't have time for your nonsense. If you're not gonna level with me, then I don't have any use for you."

"What makes you think I know anything?"

"Just a hunch. I'm gonna give you one last chance. For your sake, I hope you take it. Because if you tell me again that you don't know anything, I'm just gonna drop you here and find someone else who will be smart enough to take the opportunity that you're not."

"You know what happens to people who snitch, man?"

"Nothing," Thrower answered, taking his gun off the man's back. "Because nobody else is gonna find out about it. As soon as you tell me what I want to know, you'll be gone, and nobody will ever see you. And I'm sure as hell not gonna tell anybody. Then you can get back to peddling your junk to teenagers."

"Hey, they're old enough to make up their own minds."

"I don't care about that right now. I need to find this girl. And the people that own that white van took her."

The man looked back at him. "The people in that van, huh?" He stroked his chin.

"That's right. They've also killed someone."

The man shot him another look, his eyes widening. He then started rubbing around his mouth, looking like he was struggling with his decision on whether to tell Thrower what he knew.

"And I don't have all night," Thrower said.

The man cleared his throat. "Uh, let's say I do know something. What's, uh, what's in it for me?"

"No bullets."

Thrower couldn't make the implication any clearer than that. That's all he was going to offer. The man could leave in the same manner that he came. In one piece.

"No bullets. Well, I mean, I guess that's a start."

"That's the end," Thrower said. "It's not a negotiation. You tell me about that van, or you leave here with more holes than you started with. That's it. Take it or leave it."

"Well, I guess if you're gonna put it that way. I guess I'll take it."

"Start talking. What do you know about the people who own that van?"

"Four guys, I think. Don't know their names or nothing. But I've seen them around."

"How long have they been here?" Thrower asked.

"Couple of months, I think. Maybe longer. Not sure. I know it's been a while."

"Where do they live?"

"Um, I'm not sure."

Thrower could tell he was stalling. He gave the man a hard shove in the back, just letting him know there would still be consequences.

"Uh, that building over there, man." He pointed to the second building to the end on the right.

Thrower looked through the bushes, seeing where the man had pointed. "Second to last on the end?"

"Yeah."

"They all live there?"

"That I don't know. I've just seen a couple of them go from the van to inside that place. Don't know if they live there or just visiting."

"You said four guys?" Thrower asked. That was a new number for him. He'd only ever seen the three. The same three in every spot he came across them.

"Yeah. I mean, maybe there's more, I don't know. But the one day last week I saw the four of them go in."

"They have anything with them?"

"Yeah. Lunch."

"You see a kid in the last day?"

"Dude, I ain't even been around here in three or four days. They could have an elephant with them, I wouldn't know."

"Let me see your wallet," Thrower said.

"What?"

"Your wallet." He stuck his hand out.

"What for? You gonna rob me, too?"

"I wanna see something."

The man looked down at the gun that was still in Thrower's hand. That was always the most convincing argument to be made. He complied with Thrower's wishes and handed him his wallet. All Thrower was looking for was the man's identification. He didn't even check for money or anything else. Once Thrower saw what he wanted to see, he handed the wallet back to the man.

"What was that about?"

"Now I know where you live," Thrower answered. "So if I find out that you're lying to me here, you're gonna find me visiting at some point. And we will finish this conversation in a different way."

"I'm not lying, man. You made it clear enough. I definitely don't wanna be meeting up with you again. Everything I've said is the truth."

"Fine. I'll take your word for it. But you'll see me again if things don't go well."

"Like I said, I got it. I told you where they are, what happens after that, that's on you. Leave me out of it."

"As long as they're there, you're fine."

"Good enough for me."

"What about how to get in there?" Thrower asked. "Any ideas?"

"What am I, an engineer?"

"Architect."

"Whatever. What makes you think I know how to sneak around and get in buildings?"

"Well, considering your profession, I figure you've had to do it from time to time."

The man sighed. It wasn't far from the truth. "Yeah, but I never had to get in that one before."

"Back door, fire escape ladder, roof, what?" Thrower asked.

"I don't know, man! I ain't no James Bond or nothin'!"

"You've never been in the back of these buildings?"

The man sighed, feeling like this was never going to end. "Can I go now? I told you what you wanted to know."

"As soon as you tell me how to get in there," Thrower said. "I know you know."

"Man, you're killing me."

"Not yet."

The man sighed again, this time louder to further illustrate his frustration with the predicament he was in. Not that Thrower cared whether he was unhappy or not.

"Just tell me how to get in without them seeing me and you can go," Thrower said.

"Now it has to be without them seeing you? What am I, a magician?"

"I don't know. Are you?"

"No!"

"Just tell me how to get in there without going through the front door. Or being spotted."

"If I tell you where to go, can I then go?"

Thrower nodded. "Absolutely."

"I can tell you how to get in. Whether you get spotted or not... that's on you."

Thrower shrugged. "Fair enough."

"All right, the front door's got that little fence around it. And most of the places around here got locks on the gate's there to prevent people like..." He looked at Thrower. "Well, to prevent unwanted people from getting in."

Thrower grinned. "Sounds reasonable."

"Anyway, there's also a back door, but that's usually the same problem with these places. Everyone's always afraid of thieves and stuff, you know?"

"I do."

"So anyway, as you can see, all these places have second-floor balconies, right?"

Thrower looked at the buildings. "Yeah?"

"So what I would suggest is going to the last building at the end of the street there, on the left."

"That convenience store?"

"Yeah. There's a ladder on the back of the building that leads up to the roof. Climb up that, then go all the way over, then drop in from the roof onto the balcony. And then you're in. Easy as pie."

Thrower gave the man a look, not sure he believed how easy it was going to be. But it did appear to be the best option. Thrower looked over at the building again. The roof wasn't very far from the balcony. It seemed feasible.

"Seems reasonable," Thrower said.

"Great. Can I go now?"

"Sure. But if you actually know these people and warn them I'm coming..."

"I know, I know. There's a bullet with my name on it. I got it. Trust me, I ain't warning nobody. I don't ever wanna see you again, hear you again, nothing you again. I just want you gone for good. So trust me, I ain't telling nobody. Have fun, good luck, adios."

Thrower nodded, then pointed with his thumb for the man to get out of there. He remained in the bushes, watching as the man went through the hole in the fence, and ran off in the other direction. Thrower felt confident the man was being honest with him. Now came the hard part. Getting in that building.

23

Not that he didn't believe what he was told, but Thrower didn't move much over the next hour. He still would have liked some visual confirmation with his own eyes before moving out. He didn't get it, though. Not from the building he was looking at.

He didn't want to wait any longer. He'd had enough of that. Thrower went over to one of the holes in the fence, away from the street he was looking at, and climbed through it. He walked down the street, turned the corner, and he had eyes on the van again. He briefly looked up at the building and noticed a light flicker on. It was only on for a moment before turning off again. But that was enough. Enough to let Thrower know that someone was in there. At least one.

Thrower continued down the street, walking past the van, until he got to the end, where the convenience store was. He crossed the street and went around to the other side of the building. There was a couple walking nearby, so Thrower sat down on the curb for a moment, waiting for them to pass. Once they did and the coast was clear of any other walkers, Thrower got back up and quickly went over to the building.

He located the ladder on the side of the building, though there were quite a few bags of trash in the way. It almost looked like a dump station. Thrower waded his way through it, eventually getting to the wall and the ladder. It wasn't the most pleasant of smells. He took one last look around, then climbed up.

He kept looking down as he climbed, making sure nobody saw him. The last thing he needed was some neighborhood sheriff making trouble for him and calling the police, or blowing his cover in general. Luckily, he reached the top of the building without being seen.

Once on the roof, Thrower kept down, not wanting anyone down on the street to see him going along. Thankfully it wasn't too long of a distance. It was times like this where he wished he were smaller. It was harder for a bigger guy like himself to stay hidden or crouch down for longer periods of time.

Thrower reached the end of the row of buildings in a relatively short fashion. Once he was on top of the building he was targeting, he dropped to his stomach and slid toward the front, facing the street. He got to the edge and looked down, only his head hanging off the building, just to make sure he was at the right place. He was.

Thrower continued looking down. All the lights were off. As long as he stuck the landing without too much noise, he should have been able to get in with the element of surprise on his side. Before moving, he took another look down at the street. It was quiet. He couldn't see anyone moving at the moment.

The only good part was that there was no roof overhang. So Thrower only needed to jump down, and he was assured of landing on the balcony. It would have been a little tougher if he had to hang from the roof and then swing his body from side to side in order to jump off onto it. Luckily, he didn't have to do that. Just a straight jump.

Of course, that would present one problem. It was a good-sized drop. Probably ten or twelve feet. And with a man his size, around six-four, there was really no way he was going to be able to make that jump without making a considerable amount of noise. That'd be a big man hitting that balcony at a good rate of speed. Maybe someone who had some ballerina training could have done it a bit more gracefully, but that wasn't Thrower. He would just have to try to make the least amount of noise that he could.

After taking one last look, the time was right to go. Thrower slid his body over the side, hanging on to the edge of the roof with his fingers. He took a final look down. He relinquished his grip on the roof and dropped to the balcony. His feet and knees took most of the impact upon hitting the floor of the balcony, though, as he feared, his body did make a pretty big sound as he hit it.

Thrower quickly removed his gun and located the sliding door. He went over to it and tried to open it, but it was locked. He had two options now. He could try to get in quietly and pick the lock, or he could just smash his way in, which would be faster, though potentially more messy, and not just in relation to the door.

Unfortunately, Thrower didn't bring his bag of door-picking tools. So that was out, anyway. Looked like there was only one way to go. Hopefully, he wasn't opening up the hornet's nest.

Thrower looked around and saw a potted plant in the corner. That should do the trick. He could have used his body to smash his way in, but this seemed better and safer. His body would thank him later.

Thrower went over to the plant and picked it up, walking back over to the door. He swung it back, then tossed it through the glass door. The glass shattered. Thrower went through the new opening and took his gun out again, waiting for some company, which he knew was coming soon.

His eyes were immediately drawn to his left, as he noticed a light turn on. A twenty-something male emerged from the hallway, looking rather displeased about seeing a stranger standing there, along with a bunch of glass on the floor. The man started yelling something in Spanish, most of which Thrower didn't understand. What he did understand was the gun in the man's hands, which he spun up in front of his body.

The man fired wildly, probably from being angry and overanxious, shooting over Thrower as he dropped to the floor to return fire. Thrower fired three rounds, all of which hit their mark. As the man dropped to the floor, Thrower remained in his spot, one knee on the floor. He was waiting for any of the man's friends to arrive.

Thrower was a little surprised that no one else was coming at first. He figured there would have been more. He slowly got back to his feet and started looking around the room. He saw a kitchen area to his right, some of which was blocked from his vision by a half-wall. He backed his way over there, all while still pointing his gun at the hallways, which is where he figured the action would be most likely to occur, assuming it did at all.

Once Thrower got within view of the whole kitchen, he took a quick peek, seeing nobody there. He then advanced towards the hallway. There were a couple of doors down there. He assumed there were two bedrooms and a bathroom. With his gun still leading the way, Thrower started down the path. Two of the doors were closed. The other door was wide open, which is where Thrower assumed the other guy came out of. That didn't mean there wasn't anyone else there, though. He had to assume there was.

That door was the last door on the left. The first door on the left was the bathroom. As soon as Thrower passed the bedroom door on the right, it suddenly opened, with a man charging at him. Thrower's back was thrust up against the wall as the other man hit him in the chest. Now they started wrestling.

The surprise factor gave the other guy an advantage, but it was his only one. And it didn't last long. Thrower had the size advantage by a fairly big margin, and he quickly started to use it. Thrower was able to get his arms around the man's neck and shoulders and flung him to the floor.

The man got up and started showing a knife, which he pulled out as soon as he hit the ground. Thrower stood there, almost in amusement, not showing an ounce of concern on his stoic face. In reality, the knife was the man's only chance in a conflict with Thrower, who probably had about eight inches and over sixty pounds on the guy.

Thrower got into a boxer's stance, as the other man leaned forward, crouching down and holding the knife out in front of his body. Thrower moved forward, only to have the other man swipe at his midsection with the knife, causing Thrower to step back to have the man hit nothing but air.

Thrower was undeterred and kept advancing forward. He made the other guy miss a couple more times with the knife. He glanced down, hoping his gun was somewhere nearby, though he didn't see it at the moment. It must have fallen somewhere behind him. He didn't want to look for it now and take his eyes off the knife-wielding man.

Besides, Thrower didn't need a gun to take care of this guy. It would just take an extra minute or two. Thrower leaned forward, trying to bait the guy into taking one more swing at him. It worked. The man tried to stab at him, causing Thrower to grab the guy by the wrist.

With both hands on the man's wrist, Thrower yanked down on the guy's arm, the knife finally dropping from his hand. Thrower then moved his hand further up the man's arm and forcefully pulled it down, causing the man to fall forward, flipping over onto his back, landing hard on the floor.

After taking a second to catch his breath, the man got up, but was swiftly met with a thunderous right hand from Thrower, dropping the guy again. Thrower looked down at the ground and saw his gun again, further up past the man's body. He went over to it and picked it up.

The man on the ground gathered himself again and crawled over to his knife, picking it up. They both stood there, like they were in a standoff or an Old West gunfight.

Thrower pointed at the man with his left hand. "Put the knife down."

Thrower wasn't sure if the man understood English, or whether he was just ignoring him, but it really didn't matter. The man didn't comply. Instead, he reared his hand back, as though he was about to throw the knife. Thrower brought his gun up and fired two times, which was all it took to put the man down.

Thrower sighed. It wasn't what he wanted to do. Not only did he not like killing people if he could avoid it, he also now missed out on some potentially valuable intel. If the man would have complied, Thrower could have interrogated him and found out about the others. Of course, that was still assuming they were not there.

Thrower continued his search, but wasn't confident he would find anything in the other bedroom. After all, if they were there, he figured they would have tried to help in eliminating him. Since they hadn't, Thrower assumed nobody else was there.

Still, Thrower proceeded and checked the bedroom that was already open. His hope was that he would find Rosa hiding in a closet or under a bed. Not in that room, though. Thrower's search of the room came up empty. No Rosa. But no other bad guys, either.

Thrower then went into the other bedroom, slowly opening the door in case there was another surprise waiting for him. There wasn't. Thrower searched the room, but just like the other one, it was clean. He left, then checked the bathroom, just in case Rosa may have been hiding in the bathtub. He was disappointed to find that she wasn't there. She wasn't anywhere in the place.

Thrower went back into the other rooms, trying to find some clue that Rosa had actually been there. He wasn't sure what good it would do, other than confirming he was in the right spot. It wouldn't confirm whether she was still alive or not. It didn't matter, though, as there wasn't the slightest of hints that she had been there.

Thrower went around the place, not only looking for hints that Rosa had been there, but also any evidence about the rest of the group. Where they might be, where they might go, any other apartments they might have, anything at all. He then glanced down at the two dead bodies, studying their faces. They weren't familiar. They weren't the same ones that he'd tangled with before. That only brought up more questions. Were they involved in this at all? Did the group have more men than they initially thought? And if so, how many more were there?

One thing was for sure, the dead men weren't on the straight and narrow. Even if they weren't involved in the kidnapping or threats, they obviously weren't the peaceful types. Thrower didn't have time to lament over the situation. He picked his head up, hearing the sound of police sirens. It sounded like they were close.

Thrower obviously couldn't be sure whether they were coming for him, but he couldn't take that chance.

He had to get out of there. Going out the way he came in wasn't an option. He wouldn't be able to jump up to the roof again. It was too high. He went over to the door and opened it. After taking a quick peek to make sure no one was out there, he bolted out the door.

He went down a hallway, then found some stairs that led down to the back door. Thrower rushed down, eventually finding another door. It led to the back. Thrower opened it, noticing a small patch of green grass that seemed to lead down the entire length of the buildings. There was nobody else out there, so Thrower left. He could hear the sirens getting louder.

Since the building to his right was at the end of the street, Thrower went that way, quickly getting back to a sidewalk. He just started walking, crossing the street toward where the abandoned manufacturing business was. Seconds later, a few police cars zoomed past him. He took a look back, noticing them pulling onto the same street that he left. Thrower sped up his walking in order to get back to his car so he could get out of there.

Thrower made it back to his car and started driving away, but he couldn't call this a victory. At best, all he did was take out two of the kidnappers' group. Though maybe that would come in useful later by not having to deal with them in a battle, but it sure didn't feel like much of a consolation prize at the moment. He didn't get what he came for.

As Thrower pulled through the gate, he could see everyone by the front door. They were waiting for him, hopeful looks on their faces. He knew he'd be disappointing them soon enough. He drove up to the house and parked. As he got out, he instantly locked eyes with them and shook his head. Angelina dropped to her knees. She'd been so hopeful that Thrower would be successful in bringing her daughter back.

"What happened?" Ortiz asked. "Were they not there?"

Thrower rubbed the top of his head. "Well, a couple of them were there. I mean, I guess it was them. Two guys. Haven't seen either of them before."

"Was Rosa there?"

Thrower shrugged. "I don't know. Maybe she was there at some point. Not when I got there, though. There was no sign of her. Just the two guys."

"Were they able to tell you anything?"

"Well, we didn't really have much time to talk. They came up fighting as soon as they saw me."

"Did they get away?"

"They're dead," Thrower replied.

"No sign of Rosa?" Angelina asked.

A sorrowful look came over Thrower's face. "No. I'm sorry."

"Where did they go?" Ortiz asked. "Was the van there?"

"Yeah, the van was there. No one we know from the group, though. They must have switched to another car."

"What do we do now?"

"The only thing we can do is wait," Thrower said. "Wait for them to call and set up the next meeting."

"And then?"

"And then we pounce."

24

Thrower eagerly went outside, seeing Recker's rental car drive up to the house. As Recker got out, Thrower went over to the car to greet him with a handshake.

"Anything yet?" Recker asked.

"Still waiting on the next phone call. Figure it should come soon."

"Shame about last night. Hopefully we can wrap this up today."

"That's what I'm hoping for," Thrower said.

Thrower led Recker inside, introducing him to everyone.

"You are a man used to these types of things?" Ortiz asked.

"More than a person probably should be," Recker answered.

"I'll pray that you don't end up like the last person

The Bodyguard

who accompanied me to one of these meetings."

Recker grinned, appreciating the thought, even if he believed it was unnecessary. "A little prayer sure can't hurt."

Recker answered a few more questions, not that it wasn't anything that Thrower hadn't already discussed with them. After several minutes, Thrower was able to pull Recker away from the group, as they went to the corner of the room to talk about things privately. It was mostly a strategy discussion. They wanted to know what they would do under different circumstances, running through various scenarios.

After an hour, their talk was interrupted. Ortiz' phone rang, which he quickly answered.

"Yes?"

"Do you have the money?" It was the same voice as before.

"Yes," Ortiz answered. "I picked it up this morning."

"Good. Same as last time. Just start driving. We'll let you know where to go."

"Fine."

"Once again, leave the big guy behind."

"I will."

As Ortiz hung up and put his phone away, Thrower noticed something different about this conversation.

"They're not watching."

"What?" Ortiz asked.

"They're not watching you yet."

"How can you be sure?"

"They asked if you had the money," Thrower said. "If they were watching, they would've already known that."

"That's a good pickup," Recker said.

"What difference does it make?" Ortiz asked.

"Maybe nothing in the long run," Thrower said. "But it could give us a good opportunity now."

"How so?"

Thrower looked at his friend. "They don't know your car yet. I could follow in your car, and they shouldn't be able to pick me out."

Recker nodded. "That works. We got another car to use?"

"Take mine," Espinoza said, handing his keys over.

Ortiz took a deep breath, hoping they wouldn't run into the same problems they had yesterday. He wasn't sure if he could go through that again. He looked at his new bodyguard.

"Are you ready?"

Recker smiled, not appearing nervous at all. "Whenever you are."

Ortiz kissed his wife goodbye, spoke with Angelina, then left with Recker right behind him. Thrower started to follow, but felt a tug at his arm.

"Please bring her back," Angelina said.

Thrower tried to give her a comforting smile. He put his hand on hers. "If she's there, we'll get her. I promise."

Before getting in Espinoza's vehicle, Recker went

over to his and removed a bag. He set it on the ground and opened it, handing Thrower an ear communication device and a Bluetooth collar to wear under their shirts, that way they could communicate without wires or phones. They tested it to make sure it was working and they could both hear. Recker then pulled out another device and handed it to Thrower. It was something they had talked about before.

"I've got one, too. So whichever one of us is closer."

"Assuming one of us can get there," Thrower said.

"We'll find a way. Just remember, if this goes down the way we think it might, one of them has to live."

Thrower nodded. "We'll make it work."

Recker then tossed Thrower the keys to his rental. Recker and Ortiz got into Espinoza's vehicle, while Thrower got into the rental. If it was anything like the previous day, they knew this might take a while. And it did. The same as before, the kidnappers called with instructions, sending Recker and Ortiz to various places, only to tell them to go somewhere else right after that. Only this time, Thrower had his eyes on them. He also thought he detected something else.

"Hey, Mike, you read me?"

"I got you," Recker replied.

"Pretty sure I've got eyes on a car that's tailing you."

Recker looked in his rearview mirror. He didn't see anything. "What do you have?"

"There's a black, four-door sedan that's been

following you for the last fifteen minutes. Even stopping at the same places."

"I haven't picked anything up."

"That's because they're staying behind," Thrower said. "They're only a car or two ahead of me. They're keeping their distance."

"They spot you?"

"No, I'm good."

"All right. I'll keep my eyes out for it."

The charade continued for another forty-five minutes, with Recker being led to a couple more places. They were ready for it, though. Eventually, they were told to stop on the side of a road.

"This is the same spot as yesterday," Ortiz said. "I got a call, then a man got into the back seat."

Recker instantly started looking into the mirrors, expecting to see someone any second. Then Ortiz' phone rang again, which he quickly answered.

"Good to see you've made it."

"Can we please just stop the games and make the exchange?" Ortiz asked. "I've done everything you've asked throughout this entire process."

Recker then caught wind of a guy trying to sneak up on the car, coming up on Ortiz' side. Recker locked all the doors to prevent the man from getting in. He just wanted to irritate them a little first. The man tried getting in, pulling on the handle several times. He then angrily pounded on the window.

"What's going on?" the voice said

"Oh, is he for us?" Recker asked. "I had no idea. I thought he might have been a robber." Recker looked at the man outside the car and smiled, putting his finger in the air to indicate he needed a second.

Once the doors unlocked, the man got in, though he didn't look so happy about waiting.

"Everything is good," Ortiz said. "Your man is in."

"Good. He'll tell you where to go from here."

"Very well. Can I speak with Rosa?"

The man hung up, with Ortiz not sure if the man heard his request or if he just ignored it. Either way, it was upsetting not to hear his daughter's voice again. The man in the back seat tapped Recker's shoulder. Recker turned around. The man put his hand out and said something in Spanish, which Recker fully understood, but pretended he didn't.

"What?"

"Gun," the man said.

"Oh." Recker removed his gun and handed it over. It didn't matter. He always had a backup. And sometimes a backup for the backup.

"Now drive."

"Where to?"

"Just drive," the man said.

There was definitely some agitation in his voice. But that was always part of Recker's plan. Usually, the madder someone got, the worse they fought. They let their emotions get the better of them instead of thinking calmly and rationally. Sometimes that made all the difference, especially when the margins of life and death were slim.

In this case, Recker started driving. He'd accomplished what he'd wanted by getting the man irritated. The man in the back seat directed them on which way to go for the next hour. It was a little longer than what had happened yesterday. If there was any thought about them going back to the same spot as they had before, that was now out of the question. They were well past that location.

"So where we heading?" Recker asked. He didn't get a reply at first. "What was that?"

"Just drive," the man in back replied.

"No hints?"

"Just drive, man, or you ain't gonna make it there."

"Sounds like a threat. Are you threatening me?"

The man grunted, growing increasingly unhappy by the second. He then tapped Ortiz on the arm. "Hey, get your man in order. I ain't got time for this."

Ortiz turned his head toward Recker and gave him a motion with his hand, not entirely sure what he should be doing. He figured Recker was a professional and knew what he was doing, though Ortiz didn't know what that was. Recker gave him a nod, letting him know it was OK.

They drove for another fifteen minutes. Recker figured he'd try his hand at annoying the man some more.

"Hey, are we getting there soon? Because I think I

might have to stop for gas soon. I mean, you really should let us know exactly how far we're going. If I'd known I was taking a five-hour drive, I would've gassed the car up before leaving."

The man didn't reply. Recker looked in the mirror and smirked, seeing that the man appeared to be more annoyed than before. He seemed to be talking to himself.

"Should I head to the gas station?" Recker asked.

The man rolled his eyes and shook his head. "We're almost there."

"Almost as in a few minutes, or almost as in an hour?"

The man sighed, his face turning red. "Two or three minutes."

"Oh. Great. Thanks."

Once they drove for three more minutes, the man instructed Recker to turn into an old gas station. There were no cars to be seen anywhere, and the building looked like half the roof had caved in. Recker had seen this movie before.

"Go around back," the man in back said.

Recker nodded, complying with the directive. Once they drove around to the back, Recker started to open the door.

"Not yet."

"What, I can't get out and stretch my legs?" Recker asked.

"Keep with the mouth and you'll be stretched permanently. Understand?"

"Oh, I do. Yep."

Recker looked in the mirror just in time to see Thrower's car drive by the place.

"We can get out now."

Recker looked around but didn't see anyone. Not even a car. He figured his friend in the back was trying to turn the tables in being difficult. Maybe he wanted to be the one to say when they could get out. Either way, Recker and Ortiz complied. They all walked to the front of the car and stood there by the hood.

"Is something supposed to happen now?" Recker asked.

"Just shut up and wait," the other man replied.

It was only a few seconds later that they finally saw another vehicle approach. It was a black SUV, and it pulled into the gas station. Recker grinned as he kept his eyes on the vehicle as it came to a stop.

"This is where the fun begins."

25

Two men get out of the black SUV. Recker leaned over and whispered in Ortiz' ear.

"These the same jokers as yesterday?"

Ortiz nodded.

"Stop talking," the man from the back seat said.

Recker gave him an evil glance, but then focused his attention on the two men approaching.

"Manuel," the leader said with a smile. His arms were held out wide, as if they were old friends who hadn't seen each other in a while. "Good to see you again. Do you remember me yet? Have you been thinking about it?"

"Yes," Ortiz answered. "But I still don't remember you."

The leader continued smiling, as if he was amused by it all. "You keep thinking about it. One day it will come to you."

"Perhaps."

"Enough of the small talk, huh? I'm sure we're all eager to complete this transaction, right?" He looked at Recker. "I see you've brought a new friend with you. Do you really think it was necessary?"

Ortiz shrugged.

"Did he tell you what happened to the last guy?" he said with a laugh.

Recker grinned. "Sure did."

The wide smile didn't leave the leader's face. "Ah, a confident man, you are, huh? No worries. Tough."

"Something like that."

"Well, I assume you brought the money?"

Recker grabbed Ortiz' arm before he turned to get the briefcase from the car. "Before he does that, we need to see the girl."

"The girl? What, you don't trust me?"

Recker stared at him, then slowly shook his head. "Not really."

The leader laughed. "That's not how this works. I am in charge here. I say what happens, not you."

"We see the girl, or you don't get the money."

The leader took a step back, sizing up the new bodyguard. He had a confident personality. There was no disputing that. Different from the guard from the day before.

"I have his gun," the man behind Recker said, holding Recker's gun up high for the leader to see.

"Tell me," the leader said. "Why should I even

The Bodyguard

stand here for a second longer and negotiate with you? I could kill you both right now and take the money without even a second thought if I wanted to."

Recker shook his head. "I don't think so."

The leader began laughing again. "Oh, no? Really? Tell me why?"

Recker looked down at the man's shirt, seeing the red dot from Thrower's rifle. "Because you're not in command of this situation."

"Oh yeah? And who is? You?"

Recker laughed along with his new friend. "That's right."

"You've got big balls, my friend. I like it. I will almost hate to kill you."

"Well, before you make any stupid and sudden movements, I'd advise you to look down."

"Look down?"

Recker nodded and pointed to the mark.. "Yeah. Right there."

The leader did, more so out of amusement. The smile quickly faded, assuming he knew what the dot was from. He then looked back up at Recker, his face much more serious. He knew he was in trouble.

"So, now, here's what we're gonna do," Recker said. "All of you are gonna drop your guns." Recker pulled out his backup weapon and pointed it at the man. "Or else you're gonna be the first one killed."

"I thought I told you to take his guns?!" the leader shouted, tossing his gun on the ground.

The man behind Ortiz dropped Recker's gun, along with his own. He threw his hands up. "How was I supposed to know he had extra?"

"That's why you're supposed to check!"

The leader had his hands halfway up. "So what now?"

"Your friends are going to stay in the same position they are now. If they move one little inch, they're gonna get a hole blown through them."

"And me?"

"You are going to lead me to the back of your car, there," Recker said. "And then we're gonna look inside for the girl who's supposed to be in there."

The leader turned around and started walking back to the SUV, with Recker closely following. Once they got around to the back of the vehicle, the leader stopped, as if he didn't know what to do next.

"Open it," Recker said.

"Open it?"

"That's right."

"It's unlocked. You can do the honors."

It actually worked out better for Recker this way, as he leaned over, like he was looking for the button to open the trunk. He put his free hand underneath the bumper, sticking the small tracking device on the inside of it. Just as he then hit the button to open the trunk, the leader forcefully pushed him, though Recker did his best to make it look like he was taken by surprise, and fell over onto the ground.

The leader jumped over Recker and quickly hopped into the SUV, starting it up, and racing out of there. The other two of his men were left to their own defenses. As the two men reached for their weapons, Thrower picked one of them off. Ortiz ran for the safety of the car. The man from the back seat was standing there, his head spinning around, unsure of what to do. Recker quickly made it unnecessary, as he put a couple of holes in him.

The meeting now ended just as quickly as it had begun. Recker went over to check on the two bodies, making sure they were dead. Ortiz poked his head up from the back seat of the car and looked out the window. Seeing that Recker was the only one standing, he figured it was safe to get out.

"What happened?" Ortiz asked.

"Looks like we had a difference of opinion."

Recker got into the car. Ortiz joined him in the car.

"What about Rosa?"

"She wasn't there," Recker said, grabbing his bag.

"But what do we do now? Now the man is gone, who knows if he'll try again, and we have no idea where my daughter is? This is a complete failure."

Recker pulled out a small laptop and turned it on. "Nope."

Ortiz seemed confused at what his new bodyguard was doing. "What are you doing?"

"Tracking them. You see, we knew they weren't going to bring Rosa today either. They were just going to try the same thing. Take you money and kill me. This way, we prevented both, and now we'll know where they're going."

"How can you be tracking them?"

"I put a small device on the SUV when I went over there with him."

"And you think he'll lead us to Rosa?"

"That's the hope," Recker replied. "Now he knows his men are probably dead. Things are chaotic. He'll go back to his base, wherever that is, and probably get Rosa."

"What if he just ups and leaves and doesn't bother with her?"

Recker shook his head. "No, I don't think so. He'll try to use her as leverage if he needs it. He'll figure that's his safety net should he get caught. He'll use her to bargain for his own escape." He then heard Thrower's voice in his ear.

"Mike, I'm back in the car. Did you put it on?"

"Yeah, it worked fine. I'm pulling his position up on the computer now."

"I started to drive in the same direction he went."

"Good. I'm moving out now too. I'll let you know what direction he goes." Recker handed the laptop to Ortiz. "Here. You hold this."

"This seems crazy," Ortiz said.

Recker grinned. "Crazy, maybe. But it should work."

They drove for a while, following the trail that the

kidnapper was leaving, thanks to the tracker that Recker put on the vehicle. Recker also kept Thrower up to date whenever they made a turn. After forty-five minutes of driving, the signal finally stopped moving.

"Hey, think we might have finally hit pay dirt," Recker said. "Looks like the guy stopped."

"What's the address?" Thrower asked.

Recker pointed to the laptop. "What address is that showing?"

Ortiz looked at him like he had two heads. "How should I know?"

"Well, what's it say there?"

Ortiz stared at the laptop for a few moments. He still had no idea. He started shaking his head. "Um, I don't see how to do that."

Recker pulled over to the side of the road and took control of the laptop. He hit a couple of keys and the address came on the screen. He then relayed the address to Thrower.

"What?" Thrower asked. "Are you sure?"

"Yeah, why?" Recker replied. "The address mean something to you?"

"I was just there last night. That building I found those other two guys in."

"Maybe he went back to the scene of the crime?"

Thrower couldn't imagine the man would go back to that building. Especially now, since it was likely that there was police tape around it. Then he thought of that manufacturing business on the other side of that fence. What if that's where they were all along? He was right there. It never occurred to him that they might have had two places.

"I think I know," Thrower said.

"How far away are you from it?"

"Like two minutes."

"Good," Recker said. "I'm only a couple of minutes behind you. Wait for me to get there."

"Will do."

"What are we going to do when we get there?" Ortiz asked.

"You're not gonna do anything," Recker replied. "You're gonna sit in the car while we check things out. Then we'll go to work."

26

Recker pulled the car along the curb. He quickly got out, noticing his rental not too far away.

"You stay here no matter what," Recker said.

Ortiz still had questions. "But what if—?"

"There's no what ifs. You stay. No matter what."

"I understand."

"Nate, where are you?" Recker asked.

"On the inside of the fence," Thrower answered. "Find a hole and crawl through."

Recker went over to the fence and walked alongside of it for a few seconds, eventually seeing a small hole at the bottom. He got down and crawled through. He immediately got out his gun, not sure what he was walking into. Still on one knee, he looked around for Thrower, though he didn't see him at first. He put his finger on his ear, even though it wasn't necessary.

"Nate, I'm on the inside. Where are you?"

"I'm near the front of the building," Thrower replied. "Once I got through the fence, I started heading up to the building. Then I saw our friend come out."

"Was he alone?"

"Unfortunately not. Looked like he had a couple of friends with him. I don't know how many men he's got in there. At least two. Maybe more."

"We'll deal with them," Recker said.

"Yeah, but more importantly, I saw Rosa. She was in front of him when they were coming out."

"They're out? Where? I don't see them."

"The other part of this is that they saw me approaching," Thrower said. "Once they saw me, they ducked back inside."

"So they know we're coming."

"Yeah. We're not getting in there by surprise."

"Well, guess you can't get all the luck."

"How you wanna work this?" Thrower asked.

Recker looked at the building. He was still a good distance away from it. "I'm gonna make my way there now. Try to pick off anyone at the windows if you see them aiming for me."

"I got you covered."

Recker stayed along the fence as much as possible, running along with it until he had no choice but to run toward the building. He was surprised, though not unhappy, that he wasn't met with gunfire at some point along the way. He saw Thrower behind some sort of trailer, though there was no truck attached to the front of it. Once Recker got there, the two discussed plans.

"What are you thinking?" Recker asked.

Thrower looked around the end of the trailer, sizing up the situation. "Well, we either stick together and go in the front, or we split up and one of us finds the back door."

Recker looked at the openness that surrounded them. It was too much of a risk. "I'm not digging the back door idea."

"Front door it is. And hope that they don't slip out the back while we're going in. Cover me from here?"

Recker nodded. "I got you."

Thrower moved from his spot and ran for what looked like the front door. Recker moved his gun around, aiming for the windows in case he saw someone looking to fire. There was no one, though.

Once Thrower reached the door, he smashed the glass with the butt end of his gun. Only the top half of the door was made of glass, but it shattered easily. He reached through the opening and felt for the lock, while pointing his gun inside in case someone came into his view. A few seconds later, Recker joined him, just as Thrower unlocked and opened the door.

The two men went inside. There was a narrow hallway, and they were immediately met with gunfire from an automatic rifle. There was a door to each side of them, and they both took cover in them, Thrower to the right, and Recker to the left.

"I have a feeling these jokers are just trying to keep us busy," Recker said.

Thrower looked behind him, seeing a window. "The other guy's using them to get away with Rosa."

Recker nodded. "Could be."

"He might be slipping out the back."

"I'll take care of these guys. Why don't you get out of here and see if you can find them?"

"What if there's more behind these two?" Thrower asked.

Recker shrugged, not appearing concerned in the slightest. "Ah. I'll take care of them. Just go find the girl before it's too late and they slip out of here."

With all the shooting going on, Thrower didn't want to go out the door and run into a bullet. So he hurried over to the window and opened it, quickly sliding out. Once his feet were on the ground, he took a quick look around. He was about to run around to the back of the building, but out of the corner of his eye, he saw something moving. He turned his head just in time to see the leader of the group running toward the fence. He had a grip on Rosa's arm, dragging her along with him.

"Hey!" Thrower yelled.

He hoped that once the guy saw him, that he'd be more worried about getting out of there in one piece than he was in taking Rosa with him. Thrower would be OK if the guy escaped if it meant he got Rosa back in the process. It didn't work. The guy kept running along with his kidnapped victim.

Thrower ran after them, though they had a head start and easily made it to the fence first. Thrower just had to hope that he didn't lose sight of them. As long as he kept them in view, he had a chance. If he lost them, who knows if he'd get another opportunity at them.

As soon as Thrower got through one of the holes in the fence, he looked down the street just in time to see the black SUV peeling out of its spot. Thrower raced for the rental. After getting in, Thrower floored the gas pedal. The two cars sped down the street, with Thrower immediately gaining ground on the other vehicle.

The two cars continued their high rate of speed for the next several minutes, weaving in and out of traffic. Thrower worried about the other car spinning out of control and possibly flipping over, hurting or killing Rosa in the process. That was why he knew he couldn't let this chase escalate any further. And it couldn't continue. Thrower had to end it. Soon.

As they sped through a few more streets, Thrower waited for the perfect opportunity. Once they turned off a main road and onto a side street, he thought he found it. They had moved into a business district, with mostly bigger trucks parked along the sides of the streets. Thrower put the pedal down as far as it would go, racing to the side of the SUV. Once they were side by side, Thrower initiated contact. It was still risky for Rosa's sake, but Thrower just had to pray that it would turn out for the best.

With the two vehicles locked together, they continued speeding down the road, until the SUV hit another truck parked on the passenger side, hitting it with the front corner of the vehicle. Both cars then spun around to the side, though Thrower was able to spin his completely so that he faced the SUV head-on. Both vehicles had now stopped.

Thrower got out of his car to check on the condition of Rosa and her abductor. As soon as he cleared the front of his car, the driver's side door to the SUV flung open. The man jumped out, firing a round that just barely missed Thrower's body, but lodging into the windshield of his car. Thrower immediately returned fire, drilling the man two times in the chest. The man instantly fell onto his back.

Thrower went over to the fallen body and kicked the gun away further. He checked on the man's condition. He was dead. Thrower then rushed over to the SUV and looked through the open door. Rosa wasn't up front. He then went to the back door and opened it. There she was.

"Are you OK?"

Rosa nodded, looking no worse for wear. Luckily, she was smart enough to put her seat belt on, which negated some of the impact from the crash. She still seemed a little shaken, though. Thrower unbuckled her seat belt.

"You wanna go home?"

Rosa nodded again. Thrower put his arms out, and she eagerly jumped into them. He carried her over to his car and put her in the back seat. Once he was on the road again, he contacted Recker to let him know he had her.

"Mike, you still at the warehouse?"

"No, I'm on the way back to the house. Didn't wanna stick around with all that shooting going on."

"Good call," Thrower said.

"How about you? How are you making out?"

"Mission accomplished. I've got her."

"Nice work. What about the guy?" Recker asked.

"He's dead."

"Looks like this thing's wrapped up, then."

"Yeah. I'd say so. I'll meet you back at the house."

Recker immediately informed Ortiz that his daughter was safe and on the way back to him.

By the time Thrower reached the house, Recker had beat him there by about fifteen minutes. Everyone was outside, waiting for the arrival of Rosa. Once they saw Thrower's car pull in, they rushed over to it, barely allowing time for Thrower to put the car into park.

With Rosa back in the arms of her parents, Thrower went over to Recker, both of them looking on at the others exuberantly hugging and kissing each other. Ortiz and Angelina came over to them. Angelina excitedly put her arms around Thrower and kissed him on the cheek.

"You got my baby back." There were tears in Angelina's eyes. "I don't know how to thank you."

Thrower smiled. "Just seeing how happy you are together… that's all the thanks I need."

"You will get a bonus for sure," Ortiz said.

"Oh, and about the other problem, looks like that's been solved."

Ortiz shook his head. "I sincerely appreciate it. I can't thank you enough."

"Just glad I could help and it worked out in the end."

As the others went inside to celebrate, Thrower and Recker sat down on a couple of chairs by the front door. They were a little exhausted by the day's work.

"Hey, what happened with those other guys?" Thrower asked.

"Oh, I took care of them a minute or two after you left. No problem."

"Thanks for coming down for this. I really appreciate it. I couldn't have done it without you."

"Sure you could've," Recker said. "Even if I wasn't here, you would've found another way."

Thrower smiled, appreciating the confidence. "Maybe."

"You would. That's what you do. That's what all of us do. Find a way. That's why we survive when so many don't. We find a way."

"Yeah, I guess we do at that."

"Hey, any thought to coming back to Philly with me?" Recker asked. "We could still use you on the team. Always have an opening for you."

Thrower thought about it for a second. "I don't know." Then he heard the happy sounds of the people inside. "You guys got a good thing going on up there. But I feel like there are more people out there who need me. People who need what I can bring. This is what I was meant to do."

ALSO BY MIKE RYAN

Continue reading the Nate Thrower series with the next book, All In.

Other works:

The Silencer Series

The Extractor Series

The Eliminator Series

The Cari Porter Series

The Cain Series

The Ghost Series

The Brandon Hall Series

A Dangerous Man

The Last Job

The Crew

ABOUT THE AUTHOR

Mike Ryan is a USA Today Bestselling Author, and lives in Pennsylvania with his wife, and four children. He's the author of numerous bestselling books. Visit his website at www.mikeryanbooks.com to find out more about his books, and sign up for his newsletter, where you will get exclusive short stories, and never miss a release date. You can also interact with Mike via Facebook, and Instagram.

facebook.com/mikeryanauthor
instagram.com/mikeryanauthor

Printed in Great Britain
by Amazon